Gage tilted Harper's chin, forcing her to meet his gaze. "Two million dollars is a heck of an incentive. He'll keep Shane safe, for now, in case he has to offer proof of life. But once he has the money, odds are that he'll try to kill Shane, and you. No witnesses. Clean getaway."

"Oh my God," she whispered.

He dropped his hand. "Your father may have convinced you that I'd be the perfect fall guy if things go wrong. But you're getting way more than that. My years in the Secret Service were boot camp for what I've done since then. There's not a line I won't cross, a law I won't break, to rescue our child."

She let out a shaky breath. "Maybe this isn't such a good idea. Maybe you shouldn't be a part of this after all."

His eyes narrowed in warning. "Your decision was made the moment you told me I have a son. I'm in this, whether you want me to be or not."

KILLER CONSPIRACY

LENA DIAZ

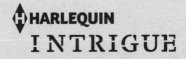

This book is dedicated to the Secret Service agents on the front line who risk their own lives every day to ensure the safety of our leaders and their families.

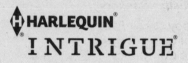

HARLEQUIN®
INTRIGUE®

ISBN-13: 978-1-335-40172-4

Killer Conspiracy

Copyright © 2021 by Lena Diaz

This edition published by arrangement with Harlequin Books S.A.

For questions and comments about the quality of this book, please contact us at CustomerService@Harlequin.com.

Harlequin Enterprises ULC
22 Adelaide St. West, 40th Floor
Toronto, Ontario M5H 4E3, Canada
www.Harlequin.com

Printed in U.S.A.

Lena Diaz was born in Kentucky and has also lived in California, Louisiana and Florida, where she now resides with her husband and two children. Before becoming a romantic suspense author, she was a computer programmer. A Romance Writers of America Golden Heart® Award finalist, she has also won the prestigious Daphne du Maurier Award for Excellence in Mystery/Suspense. To get the latest news about Lena, please visit her website, lenadiaz.com.

Books by Lena Diaz

Harlequin Intrigue

The Justice Seekers

Cowboy Under Fire
Agent Under Siege
Killer Conspiracy

The Mighty McKenzies

Smoky Mountains Ranger
Smokies Special Agent
Conflicting Evidence
Undercover Rebel

Tennessee SWAT

Mountain Witness
Secret Stalker
Stranded with the Detective
SWAT Standoff

Marshland Justice

Missing in the Glades
Arresting Developments
Deep Cover Detective
Hostage Negotiation

Visit the Author Profile page at Harlequin.com.

CAST OF CHARACTERS

Gage Bishop—This former Secret Service agent's career was destroyed by the woman he was assigned to guard: the president's adult daughter, Harper Manning. Now, as a Justice Seeker, he has to help her, and he realizes he never got over her.

Harper Manning—Daughter of the former president, she has a secret that forces her back into the life of the man she once loved, Gage Bishop. But will her secret bring them closer together or destroy them both?

Mason Ford—After his life is nearly destroyed by a corrupt small-town government, this former chief of police uses his lawsuit winnings to form The Justice Seekers. He offers former law-enforcement officers a second chance to redeem themselves and obtain justice for others.

Earl Manning—The former president of the United States puts reputation above all else. Would he kill his own daughter in order to protect his legacy?

Cynthia Manning—Harper's stepsister claims to love Harper, but is it a front to cover something far more sinister?

Julia Manning—Is she the evil stepmother, or could she be Harper's salvation?

Jack Thompson—Why is this Secret Service agent pretending to be Bishop's friend when they never got along in the past?

Randy Faulk—This Secret Service agent replaced Bishop after he was fired. Does he know Harper's secret? Could he be the one behind the ransom notes and masked gunmen?

Chapter One

Gage Bishop knew that protecting the former president of the United States, especially *this* former president, wasn't likely to go according to plan. Two-termer Earl Manning preferred his own counsel to that of others, including his security detail. That was why he and his family were in a boisterous, drunken crowd of potentially dangerous Fourth of July revelers on a Sunday morning in the middle of downtown Gatlinburg, Tennessee. If something happened to Manning because of this foolishness, it wouldn't keep Bishop awake at night. But he *did* care if something happened to Manning's family, even though he'd tried for years not to. Most days, *Harper* Manning didn't even enter his thoughts. But today, seeing her father, her stepmother, and two younger siblings again, after all this time, meant he couldn't *stop* thinking about her.

It's been six years. She's not even here. Focus on your job.

The former president and his entourage entered a gift shop fifty yards away at Bishop's nine o'clock. Adjusting his dark shades, he took the opportunity to scan the sidewalks and street from his slightly elevated vantage point on the other side of the road. That's when he spotted him: a lone male with a laser-like fascination with the façade of the store Earl Manning and his family had just entered.

He spoke into the mic at his wrist. "Zone three, suspicious white male near aquarium entrance heading north on River Road, blue shorts, white T-shirt, dark brown hair, thirty-five to forty years old."

Bishop began weaving his way through the crowd, zigzagging to keep the subject in his line of sight.

A click sounded in his ear. "Suspicious male just passed me. I'm on his six," a voice announced.

"I'm on his eight o'clock, ten feet away," another voice said through the earpiece.

Bishop spotted the two Secret Service agents who'd spoken, angling in on their target like border collies herding sheep. He stopped and surveyed the crowd in their vicinity. About forty feet back, another man seemed far too interested in what was happening. He also stopped, his head swiveling as he eyed the agents. Reversing direction, he hurried away.

Manning and his family stepped out of the gift shop. Half a dozen agents were with them, including Randy Faulk and Jack Thompson, two men Bishop had worked with years ago when he'd been with the Secret Service. Backing them up were three of Bishop's current coworkers, fellow Justice Seekers hired to augment the security for this high-profile event in their town.

Static sounded in his ear. "Suspicious male escorted away for questioning. Zone three secure."

That didn't mean the former president was secure, not if the feeling of dread in Bishop's gut was any indication. He reacquired a line of sight on the second suspicious male and started forward. The man wasn't close to Manning and wasn't moving toward him. But that didn't reassure Bishop, given the man's earlier interest. Something was off.

Bishop increased his speed, jogging as he worked to catch up. His prey was now solidly in zone five, the farthest from the former president and the least protected since the security risk had been deemed the lowest.

"Zone five," he said into his mic. "Who's covering zone five?"

There should have been at least one Secret Service agent covering that zone, per the plan. But no one responded.

The subject hiked up an incline then disappeared between two shops perched on the hill.

"Zone five! Repeat, suspicious white male."

A click sounded. "Disturbance in the red zone, zone one. Converge. All available agents."

Bishop had just started up the hill but stopped to look over his shoulder. Red zone meant the area directly around the former president. What appeared to be drunken brawls had broken out at two different locations on the street, both in close proximity to Manning. Agents were running toward the scene like ants at a picnic. Bishop ignored the call. He didn't feel compelled to blindly follow their protocol anymore. Instead he'd follow his instincts, instincts that told him those drunks weren't the true danger.

He turned back as the man he was after ducked into the doorway of a two-story building halfway up the street. Bishop took off running.

"Zone five," he repeated as he sprinted. "Request assistance. White male, green Hawaiian shirt, blue jean shorts, sandy-blond hair, approximately fifty years old." He gave the address of the building where the man had disappeared, two doors away. "Need assistance."

"On my way," one of his fellow Seekers answered. It sounded like Dalton, but they didn't use names in transmissions. "I'm in zone three. ETA one minute."

No one else answered the call. Bishop had a sinking feeling that Dalton's one minute was going to be about a half minute too late. He burst through the doorway into the shop. No customers, no one there to greet him, which had him even more concerned. A thump sounded overhead. He drew his pistol and sprinted for the stairs along the back wall.

"Coming up the hill," Dalton announced, his voice choppy as he ran.

The sound of glass breaking sent Bishop into overdrive. He topped the stairs, sweeping his pistol out in front of him. He checked one door, another, before heading into the last room.

The man in the Hawaiian shirt was on his knees in front of a high-powered rifle on a tripod, aiming it out the window he'd obviously just broken. Bishop shouted for him to stop and aimed his pistol at the guy's torso. The man ignored him.

Bishop was about to squeeze the trigger when he saw movement in a window in the building cater-cornered across the street. A child, probably three or four years old. Too close. Too risky. He couldn't take the shot.

He barreled into the man with the rifle, knocking it skyward just as it fired. The man screamed as Bishop's momentum carried both of them through the window into open air.

Chapter Two

"I'm okay. Enough already." Bishop jerked away from the well-meaning EMTs crouching beside him on the curb. "Thank you," he managed. "But go take care of someone who needs you, all right?"

They exchanged exasperated glances, but retreated toward the roadblock the Secret Service had set up. Twenty feet away, lying across the same curb where Bishop was sitting, was the gunman. He was covered with a sheet, his lifeblood staining the asphalt.

Not far from him, Dalton was talking to a couple of agents, no doubt giving his version of events. He'd arrived just in time to see Bishop and Hawaiian Shirt Guy take a swan dive from the second floor. Luckily for Bishop, he'd landed on top of the suspect. Not so lucky for the suspect.

From behind Bishop, a shadow lengthened across the grass onto the street.

"I was wondering when you'd arrive for your sit rep, Mason."

"How do you always know who's behind you? I swear you really do have eyes in the back of your head."

Bishop didn't bother explaining what to him was obvious. He'd worked with Mason Ford long enough to recognize his footfalls, even the smell of the cologne he sometimes wore. Paying attention to details like that could mean the difference between life and death, both in his former occupation as an agent and his present one working for Mason as a Justice Seeker.

"I see you refused to go to the hospital," Mason said. "You sure you're okay?"

"Thanks to the shooter being my pillow, just a few minor cuts and bruises. I'm fine."

Mason settled onto the grass and stretched his long legs out in front.

Bishop glanced at him before returning his attention to the chaos around them. "I heard Manning survived the close encounter with a couple of town drunks."

"To be fair, I heard one of them had a pocketknife. A patriotic little red, white and blue one made just for the occasion."

Bishop made a derisive sound.

"Situation report," Mason said. "Word is you saved Manning's life."

"A definite downside to this particular assignment but it couldn't be helped."

Mason chuckled. "Old grudges run deep, don't they?"

"You would know."

"On that we agree, my friend. He had a rifle with a scope set up ready to go?"

"He did. Secret Service discovered the dead shopkeeper in a back room. Their theory is the shooter killed him early this morning then locked the place to keep it clear of customers. If he couldn't get Manning on the street, this was his fallback location. Once he realized how heavily the former president was guarded, he retreated here for a Hail Mary. He may have been partnering with Aquarium Guy. That's not clear yet.

"He must have heard me coming after him," Bishop added, "because he didn't waste time raising the window. He broke the glass, hoping to get a quick shot off before I could reach him. Those drunks in the crowd had everyone in motion, making it tough to get a bead on the target. That likely gave me the extra seconds I needed to take out the shooter before he fired. Otherwise…" He shrugged. "Who knows."

"I'll be sure to mention that to the judge when he sentences them for disorderly conduct," he said dryly. "You spoke to the Feds already, gave a statement?"

"As much of one as I'm going to give."

"Understood. I'll run interference on that. But there is one other thing. I know you don't want to speak to Manning but—"

"Don't, Mason."

"Ten minutes. That's all he's asking. It'll be a photo opportunity for him, the magnanimous former president shakes the hand of the former Secret Service agent who once protected his oldest daughter and just saved his life. It will do wonders for his speaker fees."

"Not interested. And I'm not about to shake his hand, in public or anywhere else."

"I warned him you might say that. He wasn't pleased."

Bishop shrugged. "He's not used to being told no."

"Again, can't argue with that assessment. But that's not the end of it. He insists he still needs to speak to you, that he knew you were hired to augment security today. Seems he planned to ask for an audience even before the attempt on his life."

Bishop shook his head. "The last time he and I were in a room together, I told him exactly what I thought of him and the bogus lies that got me fired. Does he think I've mellowed over the years? That I won't tell him exactly what I think of him again?"

"He's being secretive, hasn't given me anything beyond the barest details about why he wants to speak with you."

"Corrupt Manning being secretive. Imagine that."

"Work with me, Bishop. I'm just the messenger. And while the Justice Seekers won't lack work even without the occasional government contract, our reputation could suffer if Manning bad-mouths our company. You of all people know what happens when you get on his bad side."

Bishop fisted his hands. Agents were still swarming the area, interviewing so-called witnesses and searching for evidence. He didn't envy whoever was supposed to be guarding zone five. Or who'd been on the advance prep team for this visit. Secret Service had insisted they be the ones to secure buildings nearby. They'd screwed up, big-time, to have missed securing a second-floor window with a direct line of sight if Manning went to any of the tourist traps along River Road.

"Bishop?"

He sighed heavily. "You're a bajillionaire, Mason. I don't believe for one second that you'd lose sleep over the possibility of Manning lying about your company. There's something else going on." When Mason didn't respond, Bishop studied him from over the top of his shades. "That bad, huh?"

Mason's jaw tightened. "It seems the former president wants to hire the Justice Seekers for a side job.

More specifically, he wants to hire *you* to protect someone. Swears you're the only one he trusts."

"*Trusts?* He actually said that with a straight face?"

"I know, I know. Given your past, what he did, what he thinks *you* did, I don't understand it, either. But he wouldn't back down. Says it's urgent. All I'm asking is that you listen to what he has to say before you tell him no."

"Is this an order or a request? Sir?"

"Don't call me sir. And you of all people know I'd never *order* you to do anything."

"Then I respectfully decline. And my shift is over." He pushed to his feet, careful to resist the urge to rub the sore ribs that had taken the brunt of his fall. If Mason even suspected he might have a more serious injury, he'd force him to get medical treatment even if he had to point a gun at him to do it.

"Wait." Mason motioned him to the other side of the street, away from the milling agents.

Bishop reluctantly followed then leaned against the cater-cornered building where he'd seen the child in the window nearly an hour earlier. He crossed his arms, longing for the hot shower waiting for him at home. It would do wonders for his sore muscles and aching ribs. Hopefully it would also wash the stench of Earl Manning from his mind.

Mason crossed his arms, too, his suit jacket pulling tight across his broad shoulders. "You did me a huge favor helping manage security for this event. Your prior experience with the Secret Service was invaluable. All our guys performed admirably, mostly because you planned out every detail—at least, what those agents would allow."

"Stop blowing smoke. Just say it."

Mason turned to face him. "Even though I don't know the details about *why* Manning wants to hire you for bodyguard duty, I do know the identity of the person who needs protection. Bishop, it's Harper."

Chapter Three

Harper headed for the second-floor conference room of the office building where she'd been summoned by her father. She forced a smile for Randy Faulk, the Secret Service agent standing guard outside the door, the same agent who'd protected her years ago, after Gage left. While she had nothing against Faulk, he'd always been more of a friend to her stepmom than to her. They'd just never had the camaraderie that she and Gage'd had. Well, until they didn't.

"Ms. Manning." He gave her a polite smile. "Good to see you again."

"You, too, Mr. Faulk. Is my father inside yet?"

"I'm told he's on his way." He held the door open for her.

She thanked him and sadly wondered why he was relegated to playing doorman for a former president when he'd earned a promotion to the coveted White House detail last year.

When she stepped inside the conference room, she stopped, alarmed to see so many people for what was supposed to be a private meeting. Press passes marked the majority as members of the media. Most of the others she recognized as Secret Service agents, having met them during her father's tenure in office. But the two men standing apart from everyone else, near one of the blinds-covered windows, captured her attention. One in particular had her heart twisting in her chest.

Gage Bishop.

She knew he'd be here. But she hadn't expected that seeing him again would make her feel this unsettled. He was still so mouthwateringly handsome that her nails bit into her palms. Her fingers ached to trace his chiseled jaw, to smooth the tiny crescent-shaped birthmark on his left cheek, to thread through the dark brown hair that she remembered was soft and thick. He was wearing it longer than he used to, though it was still shorter than currently fashionable. The light beard was new, along with the barely there mustache. It seemed impossible, but he was even better looking now than when he'd lived in the pool house behind the Manning family home in Nashville while serving as her full-time bodyguard.

His posture subtly changed moments before his gaze locked on hers. He'd always been able to do that, somehow sense when she entered a room even before he saw her. But where in the past he'd smile or give her a warm greeting, the cold hardness now glittering in his deep blue eyes had her all but shivering before she lost the staring contest and looked away. She moved to the opposite side of the room to lean against the wall while she tamped down the unexpected rush of emotions threatening to shred her self-confidence and resolve.

The door opened again. Everyone fell silent as her father stepped inside with two more agents. Just how much security did one man need? Knowing his ego, he'd probably made a special request for extra protection this trip because of all the media around on Independence Day. Nothing could make a man look more important than when surrounded by a heavy security detail in dark sunglasses with guns bulging beneath their suit jackets. It was like a *Men in Black* convention, minus the aliens. And no one was laughing.

His gaze zeroed in on Gage as hers had. But his polite nod went unacknowledged and unreturned. Where Gage had looked at her with cold indifference, he stared at her father with undisguised loathing.

The man standing beside Gage in a nearly matching dove-gray business suit leaned in and said something. Gage gave him a curt nod of agreement then aimed his lethal stare elsewhere.

"Ladies and gentlemen." Her father's practiced smile was at full wattage. "Before I answer your questions about today's events, I need to attend to some private business. It will only take a few moments. Could everyone please clear out except Mr. Ford, Bishop, and my daughter?"

He hadn't even looked her way when he'd entered the room. Had he just assumed she was there because he couldn't imagine her daring to be late after he'd summoned her? Even though she'd made the hour-and-a-half drive from her home outside Knoxville hoping her father could arrange this meeting, the exact location and time hadn't been determined. She'd still been halfway across town when she'd received his cryptic text and had driven like a crazy woman to arrive on time. At twenty-six, it rankled that she still felt compelled to ask *how high* when he told her to jump, even if his order was for her benefit.

When no one made a move to leave, her father said,

"Perhaps you don't recognize these gentlemen." He motioned to Gage and the man beside him. "Mr. Ford's company helped provide security today. Bishop is not only one of Mr. Ford's employees, he's a former Secret Service agent. I assure you that I'm perfectly safe with both of them. Now, please excuse us for just a few minutes." This time his tone brooked no argument. But it still took some encouragement by one of the senior agents, Jack Thompson, to usher them out the door.

When the room cleared, Harper was surprised to see one person still sitting at the table, her father's lawyer. She couldn't imagine why he'd be needed on a Fourth of July outing. And they certainly hadn't discussed having him here for *this* meeting.

As Mr. Roth set an old-fashioned briefcase on the table, Harper straightened. What kind of scheme was her father trying to pull now?

"Dad, why is your lawyer here?"

"Just a formality. A simple nondisclosure agreement for Bishop to—"

"I'm not signing anything." Gage straightened away from the wall. "And your ten minutes started ticking the moment you walked in that door. You've got nine minutes left. What do you want?"

Her father's eyes narrowed in warning as he took the power seat at the head of the table and motioned for the others to join him.

Harper reluctantly sat at the other end of the table but avoided the matching power seat. She preferred to blend in rather than take the bull by its horns. Facing the windows, she tried to picture the view behind the blinds: the rows of quaint little shops, vibrant summer flowers spilling over planters lining the sidewalks.

Any other time she'd visited Gatlinburg, she'd happily mixed with the tourists, soaked in the friendly small-town atmosphere the area was known for. Instead, this time, she was in a conference room dreading the upcoming discussion.

"Bishop," her father said when Gage and Mr. Ford remained standing. "Won't you please join us?"

"No."

Her father's face reddened. Beside him at the table, Mr. Roth looked as if he was about to faint. He'd probably never seen anyone treat her father with such open disdain. Even Harper's rebellious younger sister, Cynthia, didn't dare treat him that way. Not to his face at least.

Mr. Ford whispered to him again. But this time, Gage refused to concede. He shook his head and remained standing. Ford clasped his shoulder in an obvious show of respect and support before seating himself near the middle of the table. He greeted Harper first.

"Ms. Manning, I'm Mason Ford. I've always admired the work that you and your mother do for the national library literacy program. It's a genuine pleasure to meet you."

She smiled and didn't bother to correct him that Julia was her stepmother, not her mom—God rest her soul.

"Nice to meet you, Mr. Ford. And thank you."

He nodded before introducing himself to the lawyer. Then he finally acknowledged her father. Whether intentional or not, he'd insulted him by making him last in the introductions. She was inclined to think it was on purpose, another subtle show of support for Gage. They were obviously friends, in addition to being boss and employee. She couldn't help but envy the kind of friendship that was worth risking her father's displeasure. He took slights personally and wasn't the type to forgive and forget.

"Let's get this meeting started," her father said, his voice strained.

"Eight minutes," Gage announced.

Her father's perfect plastic smile was ruined by his glare. "I was going to start by thanking you for saving my life earlier today—"

"Don't bother."

Harper sucked in a breath. "What happened? You saved his life?"

"I did my job. It was nothing personal." He checked his watch. "Seven minutes."

"Oh good grief." Her father motioned to the lawyer. "Hurry up. Get him to sign—"

"No," Gage said. "I will not now or ever enter into any kind of contract with you. It wouldn't be worth the paper it's printed on." He crossed the room, surprising Harper by sitting across from her and giving her his full attention. "I'm here as a favor to Mason, not the former president. What's going on, Harper? Why does he think I can help you?" He arched a brow. "Or that I'd even consider it?"

One of the old cracks in her heart split open at the cold bitterness of his less than encouraging word choices. She glanced at her dad, who was openly glaring at him. A lot of unflattering things could be said about her father, most of them true. But when it came to his three children, whether related by blood or marriage, he'd fight to his last breath to protect each and every one of them. Gage's callous attitude toward her had him looking mad enough to start a small war.

When her father's gaze shifted to her, it immediately softened. His mouth curved in a rare genuine smile that was a mixture of sadness and affection. "You don't have to do this, Harper. We can find another way."

"It's okay, Daddy. Don't worry about me. We talked all this out and nothing has changed. But maybe you could step out for a few minutes while I talk to Gage alone. That might make it easier on all of us."

She could sense Gage's puzzlement as he glanced back and forth between them. But thankfully he didn't say anything. If he'd mentioned one more time how many minutes were left, her father would have probably dragged her out of the room, ruining any chance she had to get Gage's help.

She *really* needed his help.

Her father finally nodded with obvious reluctance and pushed back from the table. "Mr. Ford, Mr. Roth, let's step outside. Harper prefers to conduct this conversation in private."

She gave him a grateful smile as he and the lawyer left the room.

Mr. Ford wasn't as accommodating. He crossed to Gage and silently waited.

Without turning, Gage said, "I'll listen to what she has to say. Don't let anyone else back in until we're done."

"You got it."

As soon as the door clicked shut behind Ford, Gage settled back in his chair.

"All right, Harper. It's just you and me. What did your father mean when he said you could find another way? Did you learn that I have money now and you're here to extort me? Or are you here to try to destroy me once and for all by faking *another* pregnancy?"

Chapter Four

Harper jerked back, the sting of his words hitting her like a physical blow. "Wow. You really know how to come out swinging, don't you? When did you become so cruel?"

"When I was accused of something I didn't do and the girl's father destroyed my career and did a heck of a job wrecking my life along with it."

She clasped her hands beneath the table and silently reminded herself what was at stake. Their individual grievances were petty in comparison. "In answer to your earlier question, I didn't know you had money. This isn't about money. *It never was.*"

He didn't look convinced. "Then why am I here? You want something from me. If not money, then what?"

She glanced at her purse on the chair beside hers, wondering if it would be better to just show him the picture. But without an explanation first, she didn't know if he'd even bother to look at it. And if he did, his low opinion of her character would simply be confirmed, in his mind at least. No, she had to be careful, get this right. Because she knew he'd never give her another opportunity.

"It's complicated," she said. "I need to tell you a story first, one that began almost six years ago. There are things that you don't know, or don't understand."

"Six years ago? I've heard this one." His look of scorn practically incinerated her from across the table. "It's about a Secret Service agent who put his life on the line every day for two years to protect a young college student whose father's shenanigans made her a target of violence on numerous occasions. And how did she thank him for being willing to die to keep her safe? She accused him of getting her pregnant. Never mind that they'd never even kissed, let alone had sex. That didn't stop her. She got daddy dearest to pressure the agent's boss to fire him, then blacklisted him so that every security job he tried to get lasted a few weeks at best, before the lies caught up to him and he was canned again."

The bitterness in his voice had her aching inside. She'd always known he'd been hurt. They both had. But the past wasn't something she could fix. The present was what mattered, and what might happen in the future if she couldn't make him see reason. "You don't understand. Let me explain. I need to tell you about the night that your—"

"It's you who doesn't understand. You never stopped to think about the damage that your lies could do. Or worse, you didn't care." He rapped his knuckles on the table. "One of your father's minions sent a letter to my dad, spreading the lies about you and me. He was so ashamed of my lack of honor that he flat-out told me the wrong son had died in the conflict overseas. He also said that if it was in his power, he'd send me to die on the other end of that sniper's bullet instead of Shane."

She drew in a sharp breath. "Oh, Gage. I'm so sorry. I had no idea that—"

"I haven't talked to my father in five years. His choice. Not mine. And there's no telling what would have happened to me by now if I hadn't come up with the idea of incorporating to throw your father off the scent so he couldn't poison future employers against me. Still, without references, I was eventually forced to completely switch career paths to build any kind of career. Thankfully, the skills I learned working summers for my father in construction paid off. I eventually started my own construction company. That gave me a roof over my head and food on the table. But it was only when I became one of the Justice Seekers that I got my pride back."

"Justice Seekers?"

"My boss's company, the Justice Seekers. He put together a team of former law-enforcement men and women whose careers were destroyed through no fault of their own—like mine. Mason has made it his life's work to give people like me a second chance. I thank God every day that he believed *me*, not the Manning family lies."

The pain that leaked through his angry tirade had her reaching across the table to clasp his hand before she realized what she was doing.

He jerked back as if her touch had scalded him. "I don't know why I even bothered coming in here. Curiosity, I guess. But whatever problem you're having, I'm not the one to solve it. Tell daddy dearest to loosen his purse strings and hire a private security firm to protect you. I'm sure he can more than afford it. But if he won't dole out his own money, maybe he can convince his former VP in the White House to have the Secret Service protect you even though they're not supposed to protect adult children of former presidents. Earl Manning's got plenty of experience breaking the rules and he excels at strong-arming others to do the same."

"Gage, please. You haven't given me a chance—"

"A chance? Like you gave me all those years ago?" She flinched.

He shoved back from the table and stood, his expression more weary than angry. "I'm sorry, Harper. I truly am. God above knows I never planned on spouting off like this. Or being…cruel, as you said. That's not me. Or at least, it never used to be. All I can say is that seeing you again, bringing up the past, it just… it pushed some buttons I didn't even know I still had. That's not an excuse. It's an explanation. Though admittedly a poor one."

She gave him a wobbly smile and was about to try again, but he held up a hand to stop her.

"Wait. Please." His voice was soft, almost gentle now, filled with regret. "I can't do this. I thought I could. But I can't. I'm not trying to be mean, just realistic. You need to find someone else to help you."

Before she could even try to figure out a response, he was heading for the door. In desperation, she yanked the picture out of her purse and held it up just as he reached for the doorknob. "This is my son, Shane. He—"

"Shane?" He gave her an incredulous look. "You named another man's child after my dead brother?"

His barb buried itself deep in her chest. But she couldn't wallow and feel sorry for herself. This battle was far too important to surrender. Somehow she had to break through that prickly wall he'd erected between them, or they'd both regret it for the rest of their lives.

She hurried over, squeezing between him and the door to block his way. Then she held up the picture. When he didn't look at it, she shook it. "I wasn't trying to hurt you by naming him that. I named him Shane as a tribute, because I knew how much your brother meant to you." She searched his gaze, noted the stubborn tilt of his jaw. "Do you really not remember what happened between us? Not even a little bit?"

His brows drew down in confusion. But he was looking at her, not the photo. "Remember what? Remember the young woman who used to flirt outrageously with me? Remember that I rebuffed you, insisted on keeping things professional? I made vows to God and country to protect you. Allowing myself to act on the attraction between us would have meant breaking those vows. An agent who has a romantic relationship with his charge is a liability. He can't focus, can't be counted on to protect them. What *exactly* do you think I need to remember?"

"The night we made love," she whispered brokenly, no longer able to ignore her own pain, bubbling up from a wound she'd foolishly thought had healed years ago. "It's something I'll never forget. And it destroys me that it meant so little to you that I'm not even a hazy image in your mind."

"Harper—"

"It was the day you found out that your brother had been killed in combat. You got a phone call from your dad when you were driving me home from classes at Belmont University. You called your boss to immediately assign another agent to take over your duties for at least a couple of months. You were all your father had left and you wanted to make sure he was going to be okay. You'd planned on packing that night, then leaving the next morning to help plan the funeral, settle your brother's estate, spend some time with your dad before going back to work. But it was *you* that I was worried about. You seemed so…devastated."

"Don't do this," he whispered. "Don't."

"Don't what?" She searched his gaze. "Tell the truth? Don't tell you that after Agent Faulk arrived and you went to the pool house, I paced my room for hours, worried about you? I couldn't stand the devastation I'd seen in your eyes. I eventually snuck out of the main house to check on you. When you didn't answer my knock, I looked through a window and saw you passed out on the floor, an empty bottle of whiskey on the rug beside you. I debated calling for help. But I didn't know if you'd get in trouble, even though you weren't technically on duty. Instead, I went inside."

She slowly lowered the picture. "I wanted to *help* you. But when I rolled you over, you put your arms around me and kissed me and I…" She let out a shuddering breath. "I'd wanted you so desperately for so long. And I naïvely thought you wanted me, too, not some random woman in your drunken thoughts who you wouldn't even remember later. I was a fool, in so many ways. Instead of stopping you, as I should have, I jumped in the deep end and haven't come up for air since."

She hated the bitterness and hurt in her voice but there was nothing she could do about it. "Stop looking at me as if I've lost my mind. This is the truth, the truth you've denied for so long that you never once stopped to consider even the possibility that I wasn't lying." She raised the picture again, holding it a few inches from his face.

"Look at him," she demanded. "Ignore me if you want. Hate me if it makes you feel better. Blame me and my family for every bad thing that's happened in your life. But don't you dare ignore him. *Look at him!* Then tell me he's not yours."

Chapter Five

A mixture of confusion and anger crossed Gage's face, but he finally looked at the picture Harper was holding up.

She knew the moment he saw the small crescent moon birthmark on the side of Shane's face, the same birthmark that was on Gage's face. An extremely rare hereditary mark that all the Bishop men shared. She knew because she'd researched the family during the nine months she'd carried the newest generation in her womb. It had been a long trial of loneliness, bitterness and despair. But the real trial had begun the day that Shane was born. She just hadn't realized it at the time.

His hand shook as he took the picture from her.

Harper watched his hungry gaze soak in every detail as he stared at the five-year-old little boy who promised to become every bit as handsome as his father one day. He had the same blue eyes, the same dark brown hair, the same sweet smile that would break hearts when he was older.

If he lives long enough, that is.

Holding back the tears that wanted to fall, she crossed to one of the windows and peered through the blinds at the street below. She was surprised to see her sister out front, laughing at something her latest boyfriend—Dean Everly—was saying. If there'd been an attempt on their father's life, shouldn't the family be on lockdown instead of out in public? Then again, Cynthia had never been a rule follower. And she was a legal adult, a sophomore at Vanderbilt, no longer under Secret Service protection any more than Harper was.

"I didn't know." His deep voice rasped behind her.

She turned, surprised to see his eyes looking blood-shot, as if he'd been on a bender for days. Myriad emotions tumbled across his expression, running the gambit from grief to shock. He took a halting step toward her.

"I didn't know," he repeated.

"I tried to tell you. When I found out that I was pregnant, I knew it would be wrong to keep that a secret. But I didn't know how to contact you. I only told my father because I hoped he could quietly obtain your current address from the Secret Service so I could privately let you know that we were going to have a baby. I never expected him to tell your boss and get you fired, then poison others against you. He told me that he'd confronted you and you made such a scene that your boss found out. Then you disappeared so you wouldn't have to support your child."

He shook his head. "I thought you were lying about the pregnancy because I had no memory of us ever being together. But if I'd known the truth, I never would have run from my responsibilities. I'd have been there for you. For our child. I swear it. I would have been there."

Grief and regret threatened to tear her apart. There was no doubt in her mind that he was telling the truth. It was there in the tone of his voice, the misery and shame in his expression. How different things might have been. If only.

He let out a ragged breath. "I remember getting the call about my brother's death, Agent Faulk arriving at the Manning estate to guard you. I went to the pool house to pack my things. And then… And then…" He shook his head. "I know I drank way more than I should have that night. But I never… I don't remember you being there. I don't." His confused gaze bore into hers. "I would never knowingly disrespect you that way, make love to the woman I was assigned to protect, then turn my back on her after…" His Adam's apple bobbed in his throat. "My whole life I wanted to be in the Secret Service, to serve my country. How could I have broken my vows, crossed that line?" He searched her eyes, as if seeking absolution. "How could I not remember making love to you?"

Tears pricked her vision. She wrapped her arms around her waist to keep from reaching for him, knowing she couldn't bear it if he recoiled again. "As soon as I saw how drunk…" She shook her head. "It's my fault. I should have left. But I… I wanted you so much. I was young and immature. I'd had such a terrible crush on you from the moment we met and you were so determined to keep it professional. But that doesn't excuse my actions. What happened that night is my fault."

"No." He took another step toward her, so close she could feel the heat from his body, see the turmoil in his eyes. "The blame lies with me. You're right that I would have gotten in trouble if you'd called for help and my boss found out I was drunk while still on the Manning estate. And I would have deserved it. I should have waited until I'd left to drown my sorrows, or avoided drinking altogether."

He raked a hand through his hair, making it stick up in spikes. "All this time I thought I'd been wronged, that my honor was intact, when you're the one who was wronged. I am *exactly* what your father said I was. I broke my vows, took advantage of you and didn't even have the decency to realize what I'd done.

"My God, Harper. You carried my child for nine months, went through that experience alone while I yelled at the heavens about how unfair life was, believing I was the one who'd been betrayed. I'm so ashamed of how I treated you. And I'm so deeply, deeply sorry." He winced. "That sounds so pathetic, doesn't it? An apology could never make up for what I've done. For how *you've* suffered."

His complete turnaround had her world tilting on its axis. His apologizing was the last thing she'd ever expected and she didn't know how to even begin to process it. She couldn't. Not now. Maybe not ever. There was too much water under that bridge for either of them to cross. And she wasn't even sure she wanted to, not after all this time. Her battered heart wasn't ready, might not ever be.

Gage's gaze returned to the picture still clutched in his hand, as if drawn by an invisible thread. "How you must hate me to have kept him from me all this time. I've missed everything. His first smile, his first word, his first steps—"

"So have I."

His head shot up. "What do you mean?"

Memories of that awful day had her wanting to curl into a fetal position and shout her own rage to the heavens. Instead, she forced herself to keep it together, to hold on a little while longer, to explain. Time was running out.

"My parents didn't want scandal touching my father's precious political career," she said, bitterness creeping into her voice again. "He was nearing the end of his first term and didn't want anything damaging his chances for reelection. So they rented me a house thirty minutes outside of Nashville and hired a midwife to stay until my due date.

"She did all the grocery shopping. I never went into town, couldn't risk being seen and recognized. And when I went into labor, after I struggled an entire day to bring Shane into the world, the midwife said he was in distress, that he needed care she couldn't provide. She rushed him to the hospital. An hour later, she called to tell me they'd done everything they could to save him, but he didn't make it."

She clutched her hands together. "Two weeks later, I had an urn of ashes on my mantel and a death certificate in the mail. The heartache, the grief, was overwhelming. I could barely function. It was months before I was able to climb out of that awful pit of despair. But I did. I moved on, went back to school, got my masters…

"You said you started a construction company. Well, I started my own medical illustrations company, albeit a one-woman operation. Things have been going really well since then. I recently even started dating again, after years of Julia doing the mom thing, nagging me to get back in the game." She grimaced, wishing she'd left that last part out.

"Anyway, the reason I asked my father to arrange

this meeting with you is that picture you're holding. It arrived six days ago, along with a lock of hair and a ransom note from someone calling himself Sam the Good Samaritan." She shook her head at the ridiculous name. "All this time I thought my little boy was dead. Now I find out that someone stole him, and they're threatening to kill him if I don't get the cash together before he contacts me again."

Gage stared at her a long moment, as if letting everything sink in. Finally, he slid the picture into his jacket pocket then asked, "How much is the ransom demand?"

"Two million dollars."

His eyes widened. "Do you have that kind of money?"

"Not even close. My clients are doctors' offices and publishers of medical textbooks. They aren't inclined to pay extravagant fees no matter how good my illustrations might be. And the work fluctuates, that whole feast or famine sort of thing. After paying taxes, health insurance premiums, and investing in a 401K for my retirement, I've got enough left for a decent living. But I'll never get rich doing what I do.

"All I can figure is that whoever has Shane knows that my father is wealthy and is counting on him to come up with the money." She shrugged. "Say what you will about him. But when I explained what was going on, he immediately said he'd give me the money. His bankers are liquidating assets as we speak."

He stiffened. "No."

She waited for more. When he didn't say anything else, she asked, "No…what?"

"Your father isn't ransoming our son. If we pay the

kidnapper, I'll be the one to pay it. And I won't have to liquidate anything."

She stared at him, stunned. "You have two million dollars in the bank? Wait, what do you mean, *if* we pay the kidnapper? We *have* to or he'll—"

"How do you know it's not a trick? A scam? How do you know…Shane…is really alive?"

Harper gave him a brittle smile. "You sound like my dad. The first thing he did was have the ashes in the urn tested. For over five years I've polished and cried over a silver vase packed with firewood ashes." She slumped into one of the nearby chairs and drew her knees up to her chest. "After that, Dad had a private lab verify that the hair came from a live person. I have no idea how they can tell something like that, but that's what they said. Then they ran a paternity test using some of my hair and the lock of hair that supposedly came from Shane. All hush-hush, of course, using a fake name. Dear old Dad is willing to part with his money but never his reputation."

She waved a hand in the air, wishing she could wipe away her words just as easily. "He didn't deserve that. He's been wonderful during this crisis. He's doing everything he can to help me. Anyway, it's not a scam. The test was positive. He's my son."

"Our son." His tone dared her to contradict him. Gone was the anguished man from moments ago. As soon as she'd mentioned the kidnapper, he'd tamped his emotions behind the wall again and was all business, the confident former agent ready to take charge.

"Our son," she reluctantly agreed, feeling an unexpected pang of resentment about sharing the memory of her baby with him when it had been hers alone for so long. "He's alive, has been, all this time. We *both* missed his first smile, his first word, his first steps. Neither of us got to see him as a baby. And if we don't cooperate, and help each other, neither of us will get to see him grow up."

Chapter Six

Harper lowered her legs from her chair and straightened as Gage sat in the chair beside hers and turned to face her. His suit jacket hung open, revealing the pistol holstered to his side. It was a grim reminder of one of the reasons that she'd specifically wanted *him* to help her get Shane back. He was experienced at protecting people. And while it was true that others might have his skill sets, none would be as motivated as a father to save his own son.

"Before agreeing to anything, I need to know what I'm up against. I need the truth."

"The truth? I just told you—"

"Not about the pregnancy. I want to know why you contacted me about the kidnapping. We haven't seen each other since Shane was conceived. No contact of any kind. We don't even know each other, not the people we are today. So why did you track me down to help you?"

She clutched the arms of the chair. "Track you down?"

His jaw tightened. "Since leaving the White House, your father's been to Gatlinburg several times. But he's never requested additional security from a private firm until today. He admitted to my boss that he knew I'd be here. The only way he'd know that is if he'd done some digging, figured out where I live and who I work for. He's smart enough to know that I'd refuse an outright request to talk to either of you. He hired the Justice Seekers explicitly to give him leverage. Don't deny it."

She slowly shook her head. "I won't deny it. You're right."

"That means that you lied earlier when you said you didn't know anything about the Justice Seekers."

Her face flushed with heat. "Do any outsiders really know what that company is? It's not like you hang up a shingle, advertise your services. It seems like a jack-of-all-trades kind of thing, with personal security being only part of it."

When he continued to stare at her, waiting, she let out a deep breath. "Okay. Yes. I lied."

His gaze hardened. "Why was it so important to contact me, to make me a part of this?"

"You *are* the father. You have a right to know what's going on. And you have experience, the kind needed to make sure this goes down the right way. Plus, being totally honest now, part of the background my father learned is that as one of the Seekers you've worked on kidnapping cases before, cases the police had given up on. Both times, you were able to bring the victim home safely."

"Those were adult kidnappings in foreign countries, places where our government couldn't openly go without risking an international incident. It was taking too long through official channels, so their families hired us. Completely different than what we're dealing with here. You and I both know that the FBI is the agency with the most expertise in child abductions in the States. What are they doing on this case? Setting up wire taps? Working with your father to mark the ransom money? Getting assets in place for when the call comes in?"

She cleared her throat. "None of that. The kidnapper's note was quite specific. He said if I tell any officials about the kidnapping, he would…he would kill Shane."

"Kidnappers always say that. You still need to contact the FBI."

"No. I'm not risking my child's life." At the annoyed look that flashed across his face, she corrected herself. "*Our* child's life. The only reason I told my father about it is that I had no choice, no other way to get the money to pay the kidnapper."

"You didn't tell the police?"

"No."

"Secret Service?"

She shook her head. "I can't. For Shane's sake."

"You told *me*."

"It was a gamble. I'd hoped that once you realized that Shane was yours, you'd agree to help. I'm going to follow the kidnapper's instructions, whatever they are. But I also know better than to trust a criminal. I need a backup plan, a way to ensure that this Sam guy won't just take the money and run. I need to know that Shane will be returned safely."

"I'm your insurance policy."

She winced. "I suppose you are. I can't do this alone. I'm too scared I'll mess up. I need you. Shane needs you."

He stared at her, eyes narrowed, as if trying to divine her innermost thoughts. "There's more. What aren't you telling me?"

She squeezed her hands together. "What makes you think there's more?"

He swore. "It's your father, isn't it? He's the real reason you didn't go to the FBI, or anyone else."

Unable to deny it without lying again, she said, "It's complicated."

He crossed his arms, his brow furrowed in a thunderous expression. "There's nothing complicated about his selfishness. He's a narcissistic fool with one goal. Protect his legacy in the history books. His entire political career has been built on a platform of law and order. He doesn't want to ruin his precious reputation by letting anyone find out that he paid millions of dollars to a criminal." He sat forward, resting his forearms on his thighs. "Let me guess. He told you that because of my history, getting fired from the Secret Service, if things went south I could be the scapegoat. He could blame me, say I went rogue, that he was using the money to *trap* the kidnapper, not exchange it for his grandson. He'll paint me as having taken over—without his knowledge, of course. The media would eat that up. And he'd come out looking squeaky clean, once again blaming everything on me."

"You make it sound so ugly."

"Because it is."

"Okay, fine. Yes, the *facts* are what you say. He convinced me my best chance was to work with you, and only you, rather than involve an official agency. But the *reasons* aren't what you said. It's not about making you take the fall."

He cocked a brow. "Enlighten me."

"He's the former president of the United States—"

"And the reason I switched political parties. What else?"

She crossed her arms. "The United States doesn't make deals with kidnappers. If we go down that road, it will open up the current president, future presidents—all of our country's leaders—to danger. The country can't ransom Shane. We can't set that kind of example."

"That's your father talking, not you."

"He's giving me the ransom money. I owe him a debt of gratitude. God knows I'll never be able to pay back that kind of money."

"He's not providing the ransom. I am. Does that change your mind about going along with his wishes? About not contacting the FBI?"

"That would make me the worst kind of hypocrite, one willing to put others in jeopardy for my own needs. I agree with my father's policy of not allowing the country to officially make deals with criminals. But that doesn't mean I won't do it as a private citizen, quietly, so that other potential future kidnappers don't hear about it. Am I splitting hairs? Justifying my actions in ransoming my son?" She shrugged. "Probably. But I'm doing it anyway. I lost him once. I can't lose him again. That's why I need you. I need you to make sure that when this exchange goes down, it doesn't go bad."

"Without hurting the Manning family reputation, everything on the down-low."

She lifted her chin. "I choose to think of it as following the kidnapper's demands of not involving the authorities, but working with someone who can help ensure it goes as planned. Enough with the recriminations. Will you do it? Will you help me?"

He got up and crossed to one of the windows. He looked down at the street through one of the slats in the blinds as she'd done earlier. Several minutes passed before he finally turned around. But his expression didn't give her any clues. Was he going to tell her to get lost? Or was he going to become her saving grace?

"When is the exchange?"

Did his question mean he was going to help? Or not? "Tuesday. Three days from now, if you count today. He's supposed to send instructions on the day of the exchange."

"So you won't know the exchange location until right before it's supposed to happen." His mouth tightened into a hard line. "Three days doesn't give us much time to plan."

"My fault. I agonized over the decision of whether or not to involve you. My father went ahead and hired the Justice Seekers for security at today's event, just in case I agreed to his suggestion. Is that enough time for you to come up with a plan?"

"It'll have to be. Do you have the ransom note with you?"

"A copy. The original is in my safe at home."

"Let me see it."

She leaned across the table and grabbed her purse, then pulled out the note and handed it to him.

Without looking at it, he shoved it into the same jacket pocket where he'd put Shane's picture. Even though she'd scanned the picture into her computer and had another copy at home, she selfishly wanted to grab the one he had and keep it with her. Since receiving that photograph, she'd never gone anywhere without Shane's likeness. Not having it left her feeling…empty.

"All right," he said. "I'm in. On one condition."

"What's that?"

"You do exactly what I tell you to do, when I tell you to do it."

"Okay."

"Just like that?"

She spread her hands in a helpless gesture. "What choice do I have? As you ferreted out already, other than my original plan to use my father's money, I'm in this alone. I need you. I agree to your terms."

He gave her a curt nod and pulled out his phone. "Give me your number."

She rattled it off as he keyed it in. "Why do you need it? Won't we be together until this is over?"

"Not immediately. If the kidnapper has anyone watching you, and he finds out who I am, he might count that as you contacting the authorities."

"Right." She nervously stood, rubbing her hands up and down her arms. The idea that someone might be watching her had butterflies fluttering in her stomach. "I didn't think about that. How does this play out? What do I do next?"

"You follow my rules. Rule number one, trust me and no one else. That includes your father. You can't tell him anything about my plans. You can only tell him what I tell you to tell him."

"But—"

"That's the deal."

She clenched her hands into fists at her sides. "Fine. I only tell him what you let me tell him."

"Rule number two—"

"How many *rules* are there?"

"Rule number two," he repeated. "Don't tell him that I agreed to work on this case. Tell him that I refused to help, that you're going it alone, just in case he talks to the wrong person and accidentally lets them know you're working with me. Say you'll contact him later with instructions for wiring the money. We'll leave Gatlinburg separately. I don't want the kidnapper seeing us together."

She glanced at the blinds, even though they were closed. "You really think he's watching me?"

"I can give you two million reasons why he should."

Her hands started to shake. She clutched them together to try to hide her nervousness. "Where will we meet after I leave? When?"

"I'll call and let you know."

"Then…I should just…go home?"

"Where had you planned on going originally?"

"Home, I guess. A rural area well outside Knoxville, about an hour and a half from here."

"Up I-40?"

"Yes."

"Stick to your normal routine."

"In case the Good Samaritan is watching me?"

He nodded.

"I don't like this. It doesn't feel right."

"Are you changing your mind? Ready to call someone else for help?"

"Maybe. This isn't how I thought it would work."

He leaned against the wall. "Let me guess. You figured you'd be in charge of everything, make all the decisions. And once you had the kidnapper's instructions on the exchange, you'd call me to tag along behind you?"

She didn't appreciate his condescending tone. "Something like that. As you said, we don't really know each other anymore, if we ever did. I didn't expect you to—"

"Take charge?"

She raised her hands in exasperation. "I just want to make sure it all goes perfectly. That I follow instructions, make the exchange, bring Shane home. I don't want to do something wrong and have Sam realize anyone is helping me. But I'm also afraid to go it alone. It's all so—"

"Complicated?"

She let out a deep sigh.

He tilted her chin, forcing her to meet his gaze. "Two million dollars is a heck of an incentive to make sure he gets his money *and* has a chance to spend it. He'll keep Shane safe, for now, in case he has to offer proof of life. But once he has the money, odds are that he'll try to kill Shane, and you. No witnesses. Clean getaway."

"Oh my God," she whispered.

He dropped his hand. "Don't worry, Harper. Your father may have convinced you that I'd be the perfect fall guy if things go wrong. But you're getting way more than that. My years in the Secret Service were boot camp for what I've done since then. There's not a line I won't cross, a law I won't break, to rescue our child. And when I'm through, this so-called Good Samaritan will never hurt anyone else again."

A cold chill ran down her spine. "What are you

saying? What happens to the kidnapper when this is over?"

He didn't answer.

"Maybe this isn't such a good idea. Maybe you shouldn't be a part of this after all."

The look he gave her was chilling. He moved past her but stopped at the door. "Go home, Harper. I need to put some things in place. Then I'll contact you."

"Wait. I need to think this through some more. I haven't made up my mind about whether you should be involved."

His eyes narrowed in warning. "Your decision was made the moment you told me I have a son. I'm in this, whether you want me to be or not."

Chapter Seven

When Bishop reached his black Dodge Charger in the parking lot, he leaned against the driver's door, still reeling from the discovery that he had a child, let alone from seeing Harper again. That long dark hair, those delicious curves and beautiful eyes, a much lighter blue than his own, had haunted his dreams for years. But his dreams were nothing compared to the reality of seeing her in person.

The moment she'd walked into the room, his lungs had seized in his chest. He hadn't seemed able to catch his breath. It had been devastating to realize in that instant that he'd been fooling himself all this time.

He was still crazy in love with her.

When he'd been a Secret Service agent assigned to protect her, keeping his true feelings hidden had been a daily struggle. But he'd persevered, ruthlessly bottling up how he'd felt about her so he could focus on his duty: keeping her safe. Later, after being fired, his life ripped apart because of her lies—or so he'd believed—his bitterness and resentment had easily quashed those softer feelings.

But now?

He raked a shaking hand through his hair. It was

as if someone had released the floodgates on the dam of his emotions. He wanted her—*craved* her—in his arms, in his bed. *In his life*. It was a bittersweet irony that just when it seemed that he was free to pursue her, he couldn't. Once again he had to pretend to be unaffected when around her so he could focus on being her protector, and saving their son's life.

Then again, considering the trauma she'd been through—because of him and his rejection of the truth—what was the likelihood that she even wanted him anymore? Hadn't her rejection of his methods at the end of their meeting said as much?

She'd expected the more civilized Secret Service agent she'd been infatuated with years ago. But once she'd seen the harder man he'd become, she'd balked, unsure she even wanted his help. It had been like having a bucket of ice water poured over his head, leaving him bitter and resentful as he'd stalked out of the conference room. He'd regretted his actions halfway to his car, too late to go back to apologize. The conference room was probably already full of media and Secret Service agents again.

He fisted his hand on the roof of the car. It would serve him right if, once he rescued Shane, the mother of his son didn't want him to stick around. He could spend every day of the rest of his life apologizing for not being there for her during her pregnancy and it wouldn't come close to making up for his sins. God knows he didn't deserve her. But that didn't stop him from wanting her, needing her, *aching for her* so badly he didn't know how he was going to survive the next few days, let alone the rest of his life, if she wasn't part of his future.

One thing at a time. Focus on Shane, on saving him. Deal with the rest later.

He inhaled a bracing breath and opened his car door.

"Bishop! Wait up," Jack Thompson's voice called out from across the parking lot behind him. Two sets of footsteps echoing on the asphalt indicated there was someone with him. Both were jogging to catch him before he could escape.

Bishop swore beneath his breath. He should have left as soon as he'd reached his car. He didn't have the time or patience to deal with Thompson right now, or whoever was with him. But he was here representing the Justice Seekers. Out of respect for his boss, he'd try to "play nice." He reluctantly clicked the door shut and turned around.

To his surprise, it was Randy Faulk standing beside Thompson. Bishop shook the younger agent's hand first. "Faulk, good to see you," he lied. From what Bishop had heard, Faulk had done an admirable job protecting Harper after Bishop had been fired. But he still resented him because of a little green monster perched on his shoulder. He hated that Faulk had gotten to spend years with Harper, watching over her. Years that Bishop had wasted, blaming her for destroying his career.

Shaking Thompson's hand had him feeling like even more of a fraud. They hadn't parted on the best of terms since Thompson was Bishop's former boss's right-hand man. After Hines had fired him, Thompson had escorted Bishop out of the building. Definitely not one of his favorite memories.

"Bishop." Thompson smiled as if they were the best of friends. "I've been looking everywhere for you. I wanted to thank you for helping us out today. And especially for not telling all those reporters that we screwed up."

"Yeah," Faulk added. "The media thinks we're the ones who stopped the assassin. You really saved our butts."

Bishop rested a forearm along the top of his car. "Don't give me too much credit. The company I work for prefers to keep a low profile. No press interviews allowed." It wasn't an entirely accurate assessment since Mason trusted his employees to make their own decisions. Micromanagement wasn't his style. But the white lie was better than the truth—that he didn't have time for reporters because he had a kidnapper to catch.

Still, he couldn't help a little dig at his former nemesis. "Maybe next time you Secret Service boys will let Justice Seekers clear all the buildings with a line of site to the target like we wanted to do, instead of tying our hands."

Thompson's smile dimmed. He motioned to Faulk. "I hear that press conference is starting up again soon. You should head back before Manning realizes you're not standing sentry duty."

Faulk's face reddened, but he managed to keep his expression respectful, even though he probably wanted to punch Thompson. Instead, he shook Bishop's hand again. "It was good to see you. Really. It's been a long time." He gave him a jaunty salute then jogged across the parking lot to the building.

"What's with him playing doorman?" Bishop asked. "I thought he'd been promoted to White House duty." Not that Bishop kept up with the agency anymore. But knowing who they were working with today had been part of his prep for providing security.

"He made a few mistakes and is paying for it. Got reassigned to the Manning estate, mainly protecting Mrs. Manning. But as you saw back there, Mr. Manning uses him in whatever capacity he sees fit."

"Ouch. Hines never was one to grant second chances. I suppose Faulk is lucky to still have a job."

"Hines retired three years ago."

"Is that so? I figured he'd cling to his desk until someone pried his cold dead fingers off the stapler. Who's the boss now? You?"

Thompson's smile didn't quite reach his eyes this time. "Nah, that job's too administrative for me. I prefer field work, being the guy behind the curtain with the real power."

Bishop didn't believe him for a second. Everyone at the agency knew how desperately he coveted the top job. Apparently, Faulk wasn't the only one who'd screwed up over the years.

"Good luck with the press," Bishop said. "Maybe I'll see you next time Manning's in town."

"You aren't sticking around? I figured you'd be tapped for the internal inquiry into what happened. Your company is key to that since they helped with security. And obviously they'll want to talk to you since you took the perp down."

"My boss will handle it. I already gave a statement and he'll let me know if there are more questions. I've got a scheduling conflict that can't be moved."

"Ah, I see." The confusion on Thompson's face said otherwise. He probably couldn't imagine someone not wanting to be a part of something as historically significant as an attempted assassination investigation. Especially when the person in question was the so-called hero of the day. Thompson would have basked in the limelight if given the chance. The idea of not jumping to answer the agency's questions would have probably given him a stroke.

"Well, thanks again. I just wanted to shake the hand of one of the best agents we've ever had. You were a real golden boy, on the way up. No one climbed the ladder faster than you—which only goes to show how exceptional you were. Judging by the job you did today, that hasn't changed."

Bishop nodded his thanks, surprised by the compliment, especially since the tone sounded genuine.

Thompson pressed his earpiece as if listening to a transmission. But since Bishop didn't hear the telltale static typical of an incoming message, he was willing to bet a year's salary the guy was faking it.

"On my way," he said into the mic on his wrist. He grimaced, probably for Bishop's benefit. "Looks like they're waiting on me. Thanks again for what you did. It's good to see you're back where you belong, working protection detail, even if it's not for the Secret Service. See you around." He shook Bishop's hand again before following in Faulk's footsteps.

Bishop stood outside his car for several minutes after the agent left, surveying the area around him, the windows on the building overlooking the parking lot. Had Faulk and Thompson been watching from one of those windows? What was their real reason for hunting him down? They weren't Bishop's friends or co-workers. And neither had gone out of his way to speak to him during the planning leading up to Manning's visit. So why had they done so today?

Maybe he was being paranoid, especially since Thompson had seemed like such a stand-up guy just now. But he had reason to be paranoid. He had a son to worry about now. A son whose life was in danger. As far as he was concerned, everyone around the Mannings was a suspect until proved otherwise. And who better to pull off a kidnap-for-ransom scheme than someone who worked closely with the family, close enough to learn their secrets? Looking into those assigned to protect Earl and Julia Manning was already on Bishop's mental list of people to investigate. Faulk and Thompson had just moved to the top of that list.

He got into his Charger and sped out of the lot before anyone else could stop him. Once certain he wasn't being followed, he set his phone in the console and called his boss.

"Bishop," Mason's voice responded through the Bluetooth speaker overhead. "Where are you? I got stuck placating the former president after you turned down Harper's request. The next time I looked around, you were gone."

"I didn't turn her down. I just found out that she and I have a son. He's five years old."

After a long silence, Mason said, "Sounds like we have a lot to talk about."

"More than you know. But first, I could use some help from the Seekers. Is anyone available?"

"I'll make them available. What do you need?"

Chapter Eight

Harper was about to unlock her kitchen side door to go into her house, but hesitated. Clutching her keys like a weapon, she scanned the carport where she'd just parked her aging silver Camry after the long drive from Gatlinburg. The green rubber garbage can and yellow recycle bin sat side by side against the far wall as usual. Just a few feet farther down that wall, the door to the outside laundry room was closed to keep the occasional raccoon out. Everything looked the way it should. But something was off.

Smoke.

She wrinkled her nose at the unmistakable stench of cigarettes. Since she didn't smoke, the smell had her nervous, especially after Gage's comments about the kidnapper possibly watching her. Although rare, people did sometimes hike through the woods in this beautiful rural area without regard for the property they might be on. Had one of them dropped a cigarette?

Her closest neighbor, Blake Carter, lived fifty yards to the south of her east-facing home. His 1950's white-and-gray ranch house was barely visible through the trees and the sagging chain-link fence that separated their properties. Had he taken up smoking? Even if he had, would she be able to smell it from this far away?

There weren't any other homes close enough to be the culprits. Several acres of land separated most of these rural properties from each other. A deep, wide creek formed a meandering border to the west before eventually spilling into the French Broad River. And her gravel driveway was too long to allow cigarette smoke to drift up from the road if someone was passing by.

"Everything okay, Harper?"

She whirled around to see her next-door neighbor standing on the other side of her car.

Blake's eyes widened in dismay. He backed up several feet, holding his hands out in front of him as if to reassure her. "Didn't mean to startle you. I thought you saw me waving at the fence when you turned into your driveway."

"No. I didn't see you." Given his aggressive behavior over the past few weeks, she didn't temper her words or soften them with a smile. His surprising, sudden interest in her was annoying at best, harassing at worst. And she was in no mood to put up with him this afternoon.

She palmed the keys in her hand. "It's been a trying morning, Blake. Do you need something? I have a lot of work to catch up on." She shoved the key in the lock.

He stepped toward the front of the car, as if to round it to her side. "Is something wrong? You seem upset."

She quickly pushed open the door. "When someone sneaks up on me, I tend to get that way." He stopped; his crestfallen look had her feeling guilty. But in light of how handsy he'd been the last time he'd come over, the guilt was fleeting. "What do you want?"

He seemed to take her question as an invitation and moved closer. "If you're having a bad day, maybe I could bring you some iced tea. I just made a fresh pitcher and—"

"Blake, *enough*."

He blinked like an owl, a hurt look crossing his face as he backed up again.

She silently cursed her frayed nerves and lack of tact. She didn't want to encourage him. But she didn't want to make an enemy of the only person who lived within an acre of her, either. "Look, I'm sorry. I just… Like I said, it's been a trying morning. I appreciate your concern, but it's unwarranted. Okay?"

"Sure, sure. No worries. I'll check back later."

"No, no. I don't think that's a good…" She sighed as he headed across her side yard toward the fence between their properties, a fence that was falling down in many places and allowed him far too easy access to her house. Maybe he'd get the message if she hired someone to erect an eight-foot privacy fence on her side. It would cost a small fortune. But it might be worth the strain on her finances to do it.

She wrinkled her nose at another whiff of smoke and belatedly realized that she'd forgotten to ask Blake about it. Well, she wasn't going to go chasing after him, that was for sure. Instead, she hurried inside. After flipping the dead bolt, she dropped her purse onto the nearest counter then hesitated. There was a new smell in the air. Not smoke. Wait. Was that oleander?

"Please tell me that scrawny guy isn't who you've been dating," a woman's voice called out.

She whirled around, a scream lodged in her throat. Her sister stood in the doorway between the kitchen and the family room, a bottle of beer clutched in her right hand.

Harper cleared her throat. "You scared me half to death, Cynthia. What are you doing here? How did you even get inside?" She checked the relatively new alarm keypad on the wall. The light was green. It should have been red and beeping by now, threatening to go off if she didn't key in her code. Had she forgotten to set the alarm?

"I stole my mom's extra key out of her purse, the one you gave her in case of an emergency."

She turned around. "*Is* there an emergency?"

Her sister held up her beer. "This is the last brewski in your refrigerator and I couldn't find any in the pantry. Does that count?"

"Hardly."

Cynthia waved to a potted plant on the counter that looked as if it had suffered a windstorm. One of the few remaining pink blossoms clinging to the stems told her it was the oleander she'd smelled earlier.

"It's that time of year. Mom's oleanders are in bloom. You know how nuts she is about those things. She's been pawning them off on everyone with a pulse. I figured maybe you could find a home for mine."

"Gee. Thanks. I'll add it to the dozen others she's given me in the past." She frowned. "That poor plant looks ready to keel over."

Cynthia shrugged. "Plants aren't my thing." She pulled a key out of her jeans' pocket and tossed it onto the counter. "You can give that back to my mom next time you're in Nashville visiting the homestead."

"The oleander or the key?"

"Either. Both. You didn't answer my question."

"About dating?"

She nodded.

"Blake Carter is the last man I'd date. I'm not dating *anyone* right now."

"But you *were*. Mom said so."

"Weeks ago, and only a few times. It didn't work out."

"That's a shame. You're really not bad to look at when you do your hair and makeup, like today. You'd probably smile more, too, if you *got* some." She winked.

Harper couldn't help smiling at her outrageous sister. "Why aren't you in Gatlinburg with the rest of the family?"

"I had things to do."

Meaning she'd probably gotten bored and had taken off even though her mom and Harper's dad had wanted both Cynthia and their little half brother, Tyler, to be with them this whole weekend. Harper would have, but with precious little time until the ransom deadline, she'd wanted to hurry back home.

"Where's your car?" Harper asked. "I didn't see it parked in the side yard when I pulled into the carport."

"Dean gave me a ride on his bike. It's around back. He's having a smoke. I told him you don't like people smelling up your house." She waved toward the sliding-glass door at the end of the family room, barely visible through the kitchen opening.

"Thanks for that. I was surprised to see you out the window in Gatlinburg this morning. I thought summer classes were still in session." At least she knew where the cigarette smoke was coming from. Harper opened the refrigerator and took out a bottle of wine she'd opened last night. If her sister could drink before five o'clock, she could, too.

"I'm taking this summer off. Life's too short to study all the time."

"I hardly think four years of college constitutes *all the time*." Once she had the filled glass in her hand, she took a deep appreciative sip. Then she moved past her sister into the family room, only to stop at the sight of a stack of envelopes and grocery store ads on the coffee table.

Cynthia strolled past her and dropped down onto the couch. "I checked your mail for you. Looks like you're due for your annual girly exam. The rest are bills. If you don't pay your utilities by next week, they're going to shut off your electricity. Are you having money problems?"

Harper's stomach dropped. Had the kidnapper sent another note? Had Cynthia seen it? "I'd prefer that you not open my mail." She sifted through the stack, both relieved and disappointed when there wasn't another letter. She checked the utility bill before tossing everything back on the table. "I'm not late paying my electric bill. Why would you say that?"

"Just trying to get a rise out of you, sis. Lighten up." She took a swig of beer and propped her legs on top of the table.

Harper gritted her teeth. "Would you please get your shoes off the furniture?"

"Why? That table's a piece of junk. Did you pick it up at a garage sale? You should get my mom to let go of one of those antiques she collects."

Harper shook her head. "I know the rules of the

Manning household. No one touches your mom's garden, or her antiques."

"Oh, I wouldn't be so sure. I think she'd jump at the chance to part with some of her precious hoard for her favorite stepdaughter."

"I'm Julia's *only* stepdaughter. And I don't want another table. I want the one I've got. It may be cheap and falling apart, but it was *my* mother's. It's one of the few things I have left of hers."

Cynthia winced and gingerly lowered her feet to the floor. "Sorry, honestly. I had no idea that was your mom's."

Harper sighed. "How would you? It's been in my bedroom at the foot of my bed forever. I only recently brought it out here when I ordered a new chair for the other room. You don't visit often enough to know what I have or don't have."

"Not true. I noticed that ugly silver vase you used to carry around everywhere you lived. It was on your mantel last time I was here. Did you move it to the bedroom?"

"Vase?" She glanced at the mantel and realized Cynthia was referring to the urn. Shane's urn. "I, uh, threw it away. I was dusting one day and it fell, got dented. The top wouldn't stay on anymore, so I got rid of it."

"Well, if I'd known that's all it would have taken for you to throw that hideous thing away, I'd have accidentally dropped it years ago. It always reminded me of one of those things you put dead peoples' ashes in." She shuddered.

Harper's face heated. She put her hands on her hips, hoping her sister hadn't noticed. "Is there a reason you came all this way to break into my house other than to open my mail and criticize my decorating choices?"

"It's not breaking in if you have a key."

"A *stolen* key."

"Whatever. I was just curious about what's going on."

Harper kept her expression carefully blank. Had her sister overheard something? Had her father mentioned Shane, perhaps when talking to his lawyer about that nondisclosure agreement, and she overheard him? "What do you mean, you're curious about what's going on?"

She rolled her eyes. "Oh puhleeze. I'm twenty years old, not a naïve child. It's obvious you're stressed out about something. I saw you going into that conference room earlier, looking all worried. Then everyone left except you and that hot Secret Service guy who used to guard you when you lived in Nashville and I was stuck in DC with my mom and your dad. What was his name? Monk? Cardinal? One of those religious titles."

"Bishop. His first name is Gage."

Cynthia smirked. "*Gage*. Like the tool a mechanic uses? No wonder everyone calls him by his last name."

A flash of annoyance had Harper crossing her arms. "It's spelled differently. Is there a point to this conversation?"

"Are you dating him? Is that why you left Gatlinburg without even saying hi to my mom? So you could get naked with hot preacher guy and explore the Big O?"

"Good grief. And it's Bishop, not preacher guy."

"He *is* hot. You can't deny that."

Harper sighed. "I'm not denying it. But that doesn't mean that we're going to get naked and have *orgasms* together." At Cynthia's raised eyebrows, she said, "You thought I didn't know what the Big O was?"

"I was worried you didn't. Guess I figured that one day I'd have to sit you down and explain the facts of life. You don't get out much."

"We are *not* discussing my love life."

"What love life?"

"Cynthia—"

"Okay, okay."

Harper carefully lowered herself onto the couch so she wouldn't slosh her wine out of the glass, then rested her free arm across her eyes.

"Harper?"

"Hmm?"

"If you're not going to jump his bones, can I? I mean, have you seen his shoes? What are they, a size twelve? You know what that means. He must have a really big—"

"Enough!" She dropped her arm and shot her sister a reproachful glance.

Cynthia grinned. "Admit it. You've missed me."

Harper set her wineglass on the end table. "God help me, I have. Get over here you little devil."

They wrapped each other in a tight hug. Harper held on longer than her sister probably wanted, but she'd needed that hug far more than she'd realized. When she let go, she kept her arm around her sister's waist and they both leaned back against the cushions.

"I'm sorry I didn't see your mom before I left Gatlinburg," Harper said. "That was rude. I should have sought her out. Please tell her I'm sorry, that I'll visit her soon."

"To give her back her key?"

She smiled. "Is that why you took it? To force me to visit y'all in Nashville?"

"I would never be that devious." But the look on her sister's face told Harper that's exactly why'd she'd taken it.

"When you graduate college and get settled in your career—whatever that ends up being—I hope you find the love of your life. Then I hope you have lots and lots of babies." She rolled her head on the cushion to look at her sister. "And every single one of them is exactly like you."

Cynthia gave her a horrified look. "Now that's just downright mean."

They both laughed and, for the next few minutes, they were content to sit together in peace. A rarity with the two of them. Normally they were either fighting or Cynthia was playing some kind of practical joke on her.

"Don't worry about my mom," Cynthia finally said. "I don't think she even realized you were in town. She won't find out from me. And your dad is so busy lapping up all the media attention that he probably already forgot about your visit." She arched a brow. "Why *did* you meet with that Bishop guy? Isn't he the one who messed up and had to be replaced by Faulk?"

She frowned at her sister. "Who said he messed up?"

She shrugged. "I don't know. One of the agents, I suppose. Maybe Thompson. Yeah, I'm pretty sure he's said as much before."

"Well, he's wrong. Gage is one of the most honorable men I know. He did everything exactly right. What happened wasn't his fault. But he sure took the blame."

"What happened?"

"Ancient history. I'm not going to discuss it."

"Too bad you don't keep a diary. I'll bet there are a lot of really juicy secrets in that brainiac head of yours that no one would ever expect."

"What makes you think I *don't* keep a diary?"

Cynthia's eyes widened. She jumped up as if to hunt down the diary, but Harper grabbed her arm and yanked her back down. That was all she needed, for her sister to go rummaging through her room and find the baby book she kept under her mattress. It documented her pregnancy and had a memorial for Shane in the back. It was far more incriminating than a diary ever would be.

"Aw, come on, Harp. Let me read it. Out loud. It'll be fun."

"No. It wouldn't. Besides, I don't have a diary. I'm not dumb enough to write down anything that might incriminate or embarrass me later." She'd have to remember to put that baby book in her safe. She'd never thought about it being a liability before.

"Ouch. Remind me to never let you read mine." Cynthia tapped a tune against her thigh that only she could hear. "So, back to the guy with the really big—"

"Don't you dare say it!"

"—feet." Cynthia grinned.

"I'm not discussing Gage with you."

"Then what did you discuss with *him*? In the conference room?"

"Good grief, you're like a dog with a bone. Do you ever stop?"

She gave her a droll look. "Is that a real question?"

Harper rolled her eyes. "It's nothing juicy. Just a couple of…old acquaintances…catching up before dad's press conference. Gage was part of a private security company helping cover today's Fourth of July celebrations. He's the one who stopped that guy from shooting dad."

"Wow. Seriously?"

"Seriously. I don't know the details, but I overheard some of the agents chatting about it when I was leaving."

"Super cool."

Harper wasn't sure whether Cynthia meant someone shooting at her dad or Gage stopping him. Hopefully, it was the latter.

They talked a few minutes then a tapping noise sounded on the back door. They both leaned forward to see past the opening to the dining room off the back of the house. Dean stood at the sliding-glass door, cigarette in hand, motioning to Cynthia.

"Looks like my future ex-boyfriend is ready to leave. I'd better get going."

"Future ex? I thought you really liked this one. You've been with him for several months now."

"His shoes are too small."

Harper burst out laughing.

They both stood and hugged each other.

Harper tucked her sister's straight black hair behind her ears. "You be careful on that bike. Wear your helmet."

"Yes, Mother." It was Cynthia's turn to roll her eyes. She jogged to the back door and gave Harper a parting wave before heading outside.

A few moments later, Harper stood at the front windows, watching her sister hang on to Dean as he sped down the driveway, shooting gravel up from beneath his tires. And, of course, she wasn't wearing a helmet.

She shook her head and turned around, letting out an embarrassing squeak of surprise a split second before recognizing the man standing in her family room.

Gage Bishop.

"Hello, Harper." He made a point of looking down at his shoes. "They're a size thirteen, not twelve."

Her face flushed so hot, she was amazed she didn't burst into flames. "I need a drink." She grabbed her half full wineglass and strode past him into the kitchen.

Chapter Nine

Harper tossed the wine into the sink and went on a hunt in the pantry for something stronger. When she stepped out with a can of soda and a bottle of Hennessey whiskey, she stopped, unable to tear her gaze from the insanely sexy Adonis lounging in her kitchen doorway. As furious as she was that he'd broken into her home and eavesdropped on her conversation, she was practically choking on her tongue at the way his crossed arms made his impressive biceps strain against his suit jacket. Her fingers itched to yank off that jacket and run across those delicious muscles. And she wouldn't stop there.

His slow, suggestive smile told her he knew exactly what she was thinking, and it had her belly doing somersaults.

He motioned at the whiskey. "Was it something I said?"

She narrowed her eyes in warning and crossed to the other side of the kitchen, purposely turning her back on him. After splashing some whiskey into a glass, she picked up the can of soda to mix with it. But after a moment of hesitation, she set the soda down and drained the whiskey in one single gulp.

The burn down her throat had her coughing, her eyes watering. She took several deep breaths, her hands braced against the sink. The Hennessey on an empty stomach, on top of the wine she'd already drank, probably wasn't the wisest choice she'd made today. Then again, between the ever-present fear for her son and her hopeless obsession with Gage, her nerves were tangled in knots. Maybe she should cut herself a break.

When she felt she could stand without wobbling, she turned around to confront the final straw that had brought her to this low point. "You're welcome to some Hennessey. But you'll have to make it yourself. I'm not feeling particularly hostessy at the moment."

"I don't drink."

She scoffed. "Since when, pool house boy?"

He arched a brow. "Since I found out I have a son and his life is in danger. I'm staying sober and in control."

Her face heated. Again. And now she was feeling guilty over the stupid whiskey. She crossed her arms and leaned back against the counter. "You were supposed to call me."

"I did. Three times."

She frowned and grabbed her purse from the counter where she'd set it when she'd come inside. After riffling through it for her phone, she sighed. There were three missed calls, from the same number.

"I had it on silent for the meeting and forgot to turn the ringer back on." She updated him as a contact then tossed the phone back in her purse. "What'd you do to get my address? Call in a favor with the Secret Service?"

"Something far easier than that. We used the internet."

"We?"

"The Justice Seekers."

"Right. Well, this property isn't listed under my name, for security reasons." She grimaced. "Not that it stopped the kidnapper from finding me. Still, I'll bet your Seekers had to do all kinds of searches and cross-checks to figure out where I live. How long did it take?"

"About thirty seconds."

She squeezed the bridge of her nose. "Of course it did. What about getting inside my house? My sister had a key. What did you use? Some kind of fancy picklock set?"

"Credit card. Your locks couldn't keep a determined toddler out. You should upgrade all your windows and doors for something much more secure."

"On that we agree. And you need to learn better manners. Breaking into my house isn't a way to get on my good side."

"I'm not trying to get on your good side. I'm trying to keep you, and our son, alive. I purposely got here before you so I could make sure no one was waiting to harm you."

"I guess Cynthia's lucky you recognized her and didn't shoot, huh?" She rolled her eyes and grabbed a bottle of water from the refrigerator.

"Lucky for her *and* her boyfriend."

She froze and slowly turned around. "You're *serious*? That wasn't a joke?"

He lifted the edge of his suit jacket, revealing his holstered gun. "I don't carry this because it matches my outfit."

She stared at the gun a long moment and then grabbed a bottle of pain pills from another cabinet.

After shaking out two, she hesitated before adding another. Nothing seemed strong enough for today's particular level of insanity.

"Is Cynthia having any money troubles that you know of?"

She clutched the pills in her hand. "Dad's paying her tuition and board like he did mine. He's frugal, but generally reasonable. He's not the type to lavish anyone with extras. Money's probably tighter than she'd like. But I doubt she's really hurting."

"What about her boyfriend? What's his story?"

"He's a student at Vanderbilt, like Cynthia. But that's about all I know."

"Full name?"

"Dean Everly. Want me to call Cynthia for his social and birthdate?" she teased.

He smiled. "Maybe later. Does your sister know about your pregnancy?"

She blinked then looked away. Her pregnancy—the long lonely months, the awfulness of losing Shane within moments of his birth—wasn't a topic she wanted to discuss, or even think about.

"Harper?"

She reluctantly met his gaze.

"I know that time in your life has to be an incredibly painful topic. I promise I wouldn't be asking if it wasn't important."

She pulled in a shaky breath, nodded. "I know."

"Could Cynthia have known about it?"

"I honestly don't see how. She's a lot younger than me and—"

"Six years. She would have been fourteen or fifteen

when you were carrying Shane. Old enough to know what's going on when your body started changing."

"Did you remember that on your own? The difference in our ages? Or is that from one of those Justice Seeker internet searches?"

He shifted against the doorframe and crossed his long legs at the ankle. "I remember everything about you, Harper."

His declaration caught her off guard, especially since he didn't offer an explanation. She gave a nervous laugh. "I Imagine you remember pretty much everything about the people you've been assigned to protect over the years."

He slowly shook his head. "Only you."

Her mouth went dry; a legion of butterflies took flight in her stomach. The look in his eyes seemed almost…hungry. The answering hunger inside her took her completely by surprise. She tore her gaze from his, hoping he wouldn't realize just how out of sorts he was making her.

"I, um, I doubt Cynthia knew anything. About my pregnancy. She was in DC with my dad and her mom, living at the White House."

"What about weekends? Holidays? Didn't she see you then?"

"Early on, a few times, sure. We'd meet up at my father's house when he took some time off, as much as any president can really take time off. But once I started showing, that ended. I never left the rental house after that."

"What about your stepmom, Julia? Did she know?"

"Well, yes, but she wouldn't have told Cynthia. Can you imagine? A teenage girl, especially one as rebellious as my sister, having that kind of power over my father's reputation and career? No way. The only people who knew were my father and Julia."

"You said there was a midwife in the rental with you. Did you go see a doctor, too?"

"The midwife *was* my doctor. My turn. I understand Cynthia getting here before me. She probably hit the road while you and I were still in the conference room. But how did you get here before either of us? How long were you here before she arrived?"

"Twenty, thirty minutes. Give or take."

"Now I know you're exaggerating. That's impossible." She started to cross her arms and realized she still hadn't taken the pills. She tossed them back and washed them down with the water bottle.

"I took a shortcut," he said. "Headache?"

"Like you wouldn't believe. Its name is Gage Bishop."

His mouth quirked in a wry grin.

Good grief, he was sexy when he did that. Who was she kidding? He was sexy no matter what he did.

She took another sip of water, using the time to compose herself again. "There *aren't* any shortcuts to this place. You had to take I-40, which leads directly to the road out front. That's the same route I took, and Cynthia, too, I'm sure."

He shrugged noncommittally and moved past her to look through a slit in the blinds on the kitchen door. "Notice anything after you came in?"

"Other than a nosy neighbor, that my sister had broken into my house, her soon-to-be ex-boyfriend smoking on my back porch, and later, a six-foot-two-inch man hovering in my doorway?"

"Six foot three."

She arched a brow. "Funny how you keep correcting me to say everything is bigger than I thought it was. Is there anything else you want to clarify, size-wise?"

"Well, if we're being really honest here, my—"

"Don't you dare! Forget I asked." Her face was flaming hot.

Laughter rumbled in his chest.

She shoved her long hair back, belatedly wishing she'd braided it or put it in a ponytail. "I think you were about to tell me something else I should have noticed when I came inside. The G-rated version, please."

"But the R-rated one is so much more fun," he teased.

"Gage—"

He winked then tapped the alarm keypad beside the door. "This wasn't set when I came in."

That wink obliterated about fifty of her IQ points. No wonder she'd fallen for him back in college.

He was waiting for her reply. What had he said? The alarm. It wasn't set. "Right. I remember wondering about that. But I figured I forgot to set it this morning. It's fairly new, not exactly muscle memory yet."

He considered that. "Does anyone else have a key to this place? Maybe your neighbor, Blake Carter?"

"No way. How did you know his name?"

"You mentioned it when you were talking to your sister."

"Well, of course I did," she grumbled. She'd mentioned a lot of things. Embarrassing things. Like how hot he was. And the Big O. "Exactly, um, how much did you hear of our conversation?"

His eyes sparkled with amusement. "*All* of it."

Her face heated, again, which was really annoying considering she was twenty-six and should be well past the blushing stage in her life.

"Do you sometimes forget to lock your doors? Like you forgot the alarm?"

She was about to insist that she always locked her doors, but hesitated. "Honestly, I couldn't say. Living out here in the country, with only one neighbor close by, I never used to bother with the locks. But Blake's been so annoying lately I've started making a habit of it. Or trying to."

"Lately? This is new behavior on his part?"

"I hadn't thought about it like that, but yeah, I guess it is."

"How long has he lived next door?"

"Longer than I've been here. I bought this place two years ago."

Gage pulled out his phone and started typing a text. "You said you'd never dated him. What about sharing rides into town? Maybe grabbing a coffee together?"

"Okay, first of all, it's not fair that you know so much because of eavesdropping on my conversation with my sister. Second, give me some credit. He's definitely not my type."

"You're definitely *his* type. He was like a lap dog out there, panting at your heels."

"Jealous, *Bishop*?"

He frowned as he continued typing. "Don't call me Bishop."

"Why not? Everyone else does."

He put the phone away. "It doesn't sound right coming from you. How has your neighbor been bothering you? What's he done?"

She waved a hand in the air. "Stupid stuff. Doesn't matter."

He moved directly in front of her. "This Good Samaritan person hid our son for five years and is now trying to trade him for ransom. It's likely he's got someone keeping an eye on you, on this house. And you just told me your neighbor is acting differently than he has for the past two years. *It matters*."

Her hand shook as she pushed her hair back again. "You think Blake's in league with the kidnapper?"

"I think it's a possibility. We haven't ruled anyone out yet. Mason has the whole team working on this, so things are going to move fast. They have to, with only a few days until the exchange. What's he done lately that's different than before?"

Her stomach did a little flip with him standing so close. Polite, nice, sweet Gage had been impossible to resist when she was a smitten nineteen or twenty year-old. This edgier, more confident, and oh so determined Gage was even more compelling. He had her selfishly wanting to step into his arms and lay all her worries on his broad shoulders. But she was afraid that if she ever did that, she'd never be able to let him go.

She'd built a life without him, had been forced to. And he'd built one without her. Going back to the way things used to be was impossible. Those people no longer existed. Did she even want to risk her heart with him? What if he rejected her? Again? She didn't want to go back to the broken woman she'd once been. And if there was anything she knew for sure, Gage Bishop, of all men, had the power to break her.

"Harper? What's changed with your neighbor?"

"It's just that… Well, aside from the small grassy

areas right around the house, the rest is woods. And a navigable creek on the southern property line. But the previous owner built this house really close to Blake's. That means, every time I come up my driveway or turn on a light, he can see it, if he's watching. And lately it seems like he's been watching quite a bit. He's always underfoot, knocking on my door when I get home or wanting to visit."

She decided to leave out the parts about him brushing against her and swearing it was an accident. It had happened too many times not to be deliberate. Knowing Gage, if he thought Blake had touched her inappropriately, he'd stride over there and teach the man a lesson with his fists. "He's a pest, for sure, annoying. But he seems harmless."

She wasn't sure Gage believed her glossed-over version of events. But he didn't press the issue.

"I'm surprised you bought a place outside Knoxville. I expected you'd build a house on your family's Nashville estate. They certainly have the land for it. I remember your father offering it as an option."

"Don't get me wrong. I love my family. But living on the estate, even if it was at the back of their considerable acreage, would be too close for comfort. I want them far enough away so they're not visiting me all the time but not so far that I can't drive up and see them without having to drive forever to get there. What's this have to do with the kidnapper or figuring out who might be working with him?"

He shrugged. "Probably nothing. I was curious. You said you've lived here two years, but the alarm is new. How new?"

"It was installed two weeks ago, *before* I received

the ransom note. The two aren't related, unless you really think Blake's involved somehow."

"If it makes you feel better, I think it's unlikely that he is, given that he lived here before you bought your property. But I texted the team to do a background check on him, just in case. Was the ransom note mailed to you, or left at your door?"

"If I answer that, will I get a break? Or should I call my lawyer?"

"Sorry. I can be a bit intense when working a case."

"I think the word you're looking for is *relentless*. Yes, the ransom note came in the mail. Or…well, I think it did. It had a stamp on it and was in my mailbox. I'll answer exactly one more question before I cry uncle. After that, I'm either pouring myself another whiskey or breaking out a gallon of ice cream."

"What kind of ice cream?"

"Is that the final question you chose?"

He laughed. "Only if I get a follow-up."

"Mint chocolate chip."

"I'm not surprised. You always used to keep a pint in the freezer—for emergencies. I was never sure what constituted an emergency, though."

She smiled, remembering the few times she'd been able to entice him to watch a movie or to share a meal in the main house instead of retreating to the pool house. It hadn't happened often. But she'd treasured the times it had.

His gaze dropped to her mouth and his smile faded. His expression turned serious again. "Where's the original ransom note?"

"In the floor safe in my office."

He strode out of the kitchen.

She called to him as she pushed away from the counter to follow. "It's down the hall on the—"

He disappeared into her office.

"—left," she finished. Sighing, she hurried to catch up.

Chapter Ten

After retrieving the envelope and the original ransom note from the floor safe, Harper handed them to Gage, who was kneeling beside her. She was surprised to see he'd put on latex gloves. Even more surprising was that he put the note and envelope into two clear bags, like the kind law enforcement might use.

He gestured at a folder in the safe. "That looks like it came from a lab. Is it from the one your father hired to examine the ransom note?"

"It is." She reluctantly pulled it out then flipped open the folder to reveal the baggie she'd tucked inside.

His gaze shot to hers. "Is that Shane's hair?"

She swallowed against the lump that was suddenly in her throat. "I know it sounds crazy, but I couldn't bear to give it *all* away. I'd have nothing left of him."

His expression softened with sympathy. "It doesn't sound crazy to me. Hopefully soon you'll have Shane here instead of a hair sample." He gently took the baggie and held it up to examine it. "There isn't much here, but there are root tags. Might be enough for a new DNA test."

Her stomach dropped. "I don't… I don't see why it's

necessary. The reports proved the mother-son relationship. Why run the same test again?"

"Labs make mistakes. It's better to be sure. Don't you think?"

She shrugged. "I guess so."

He moved to the desk, ransom note and envelope in hand, and sat in the chair.

"Where'd you get the gloves and evidence bags?" She sat across from him on the love seat.

He held the envelope up to the overhead light, studying it. "I always take a go-bag with me, no matter where I am. It has the bare minimum of supplies in case I have to leave in a hurry and can't go home first. Since you mentioned in Gatlinburg that you had the original ransom note here, I took some gloves and baggies out of it to bring inside."

"Gloves and baggies are the bare minimum of supplies?"

He gave her a shocked look. "You mean you don't carry evidence collection tools in your purse?"

"Ha. Ha. What else do you carry? A backup gun?"

"Of course. And a knife. Never leave home without a knife."

"That suit jacket must have all kinds of hidden pockets."

He smiled. "I use ankle holsters for the gun and knife." He ran his hand across the envelope. "I don't see any signs to indicate that someone checked this for prints, or took DNA samples from the glue flap and stamp."

"We weren't trying to gather evidence for a trial. We were determining whether the ransom demand was a hoax."

"Understood. But I'll have my team perform a deeper analysis, see what pops up. Has this Sam guy attempted to contact you since he sent the note?"

"No." She shifted on the love seat, impressed by his depth of knowledge, and his confidence. "In addition to providing security and performing investigations, the Justice Seekers are evidence technicians? They process crime scenes, too?"

"We do whatever it takes to get the job done. All of us start with a common skill set. But we each have our own specialties, too, based on our previous occupations. That's the basis for our monikers. Mason calls us his Knights of the Round Table. His company is Camelot."

"Truly?"

"Truly. Our headquarters looks just like a castle." He shrugged. "It's mostly for fun. None of us takes it too seriously. But the monikers are fairly accurate."

Intrigued, she asked, "What's yours?"

"*The Bodyguard*, of course."

"Of course." She laughed.

He exchanged the envelope for the note.

"What's next? I mean, I don't see how analyzing this stuff can help us bring Shane home."

"My goal is to figure out who Sam is *before* the exchange. Information is power, and could be the key to ensuring we get our son back alive—especially if we can determine where Shane's being held and perform a rescue operation. That's my ultimate goal. It puts us in control of what happens. DNA, or a fingerprint, could give us a name, assuming he's got a criminal record and is in the FBI's databases."

"FBI? Let me guess, one of your Seekers is a former agent?"

"More than one, actually. And we don't go through official channels in a case like this, so don't worry about this staying low-key. It will."

"I appreciate that. What if he's not in the databases?"

"There are other things we can look for, like using the postmark to help us determine where the mail originated. If he mailed it at a post office, we might get lucky and have surveillance video of his license plate. Then again, he may have stuck it in some random person's home mailbox to mail it. It's a long shot, but there are other things we'll look for, too. Like the writing on the note itself."

"Writing? It looks typed to me, like on a computer. There's no handwriting to examine."

He set the note down. "You're right. *Printed* is a more accurate description. There are regulations on printers that require metadata to be embedded within the page, invisible to the naked eye. Metadata can tell us the manufacturer, model, sometimes even the serial number of the printer used. Depending on the types of records the company maintains, that could lead us to the person who purchased the printer."

"I never would have thought of that. This could be over really fast."

He gave her a look of caution. "Don't get your hopes up just yet. Someone demanding two million dollars isn't likely to be dumb enough to make it that easy. Sam probably printed the note on someone else's printer, like a library or a business center in a hotel. A fingerprint or DNA hit is our best bet right now."

She slumped back against the love seat. "Now I'm getting depressed."

"Don't be. We may only have a couple of days. But all twelve Justice Seekers are working on this. Plus, Mason's lining up a private lab to process anything we send him. Tests that normally take weeks, or months, can be done in a few hours in most cases—if you don't have to deal with the backlog and waiting in the queue to get processed. Mason has more than enough money to make that happen. He's already hired a linguistics expert who's examining the phrasing on the copy of the note I texted before I drove up here. They may be—"

"Drove. That reminds me. I didn't see any vehicles when I got home. Where did you park?"

"On the other side of the creek that runs behind your house. As I was saying, we might be able to get a basic profile of Sam, like the geographical region of the country where he lives, education level, age, sex, economic status—"

"Gage?"

"Hmm?"

"Why would you park on the other side of the creek? How exactly did you get here?"

He sighed heavily. "I took a canoe from the campground where I parked my car. Coming up to your property from the south, even with part of that trip being in a canoe, cut the commute considerably. I told you I'd taken a shortcut. You just didn't believe me."

"Yeah, well, if you'd mentioned a canoe, I might have. That took some ingenuity. I'm impressed. Sorry for the interruption. You were talking about economic status in this profile that can be created. You mean like whether Sam grew up in a wealthy family?"

"Exactly. People speak differently based on their upbringing, their experiences. The slightest distinction in verb choice or even which adjectives are used can reveal a lot about them."

"The FBI has nothing on you Justice Seekers."

"Mason would take that as the ultimate compliment. Look, I know you're tired of my questions, but time is critical. I need to ask a few more. And if you don't mind, I'm going to record what you say so I can forward it to the Seekers. That way, they can immediately start investigating whatever you tell me."

She pulled her legs up beneath her and propped her head on her hand. "Whatever it takes. Fire at will, oh wise one."

His mouth quirked. "You're still feeling the effects of that whiskey, aren't you?"

"Only a little, unfortunately. I should have brought the bottle in here for the inquisition."

"I'll make this as painless as possible so you don't have to abuse the Hennessey." He shoved his gloves into his suit jacket pocket and crossed to the love seat. After setting the phone on the back of the couch between them, he sat beside her.

"The midwife, what was her name?"

"Colette Proust. And before you ask, yes, my father's lawyer hired an investigator to try to find her after the ransom note came. She doesn't live in the Nashville area anymore and neither does her brother, so—"

"Her brother?"

"Victor. The two of them shared an apartment in town until she came to live with me. The lawyer couldn't locate either of them."

"The same lawyer who was in the conference room today?"

"Yes. Mr. Roth."

"Was he working for your father when the midwife was hired? Is he the one who vetted her?"

"Let me guess. You suspect the lawyer of being involved, too?"

"It's a possibility."

"Do you suspect *everyone* of being involved in the kidnapping?"

"Did he vet the Prousts?"

She blew out an impatient breath. "I honestly don't know who looked into them or made the final hiring decision. Needless to say, it's not like I could run around interviewing potential midwives on my own and still keep my pregnancy a secret. My father arranged everything for me—and, yes, he likely used Mr. Roth for most of that. But I'm telling you, Colette was just as devastated as I was about Shane. Someone at the hospital must have stolen him and convinced her he'd died."

"Did you talk to anyone at the hospital?"

Her stomach did a nervous flip. "No, which sounds foolish now. But my whole life at that time was centered around keeping the pregnancy a secret. The plan was to put Colette's name on the birth certificate as the mother and then have Mr. Roth perform a private adoption to explain why I suddenly had a baby. But after the baby died—" She grimaced. "After I was *told* that he'd died, I didn't call the hospital and nullify all of my work keeping the pregnancy a secret. I trusted her."

Maybe she shouldn't have. Those words seemed to hang in the air between them, unspoken.

"You said the death certificate arrived a few weeks later. What can you tell me about it?"

She licked her suddenly dry lips. "It had Colette listed as the mother, just as we'd planned with the birth certificate. The, uh, father's name was left blank." She didn't look at him when she said that. It felt like a betrayal to not have listed him. But it would have destroyed the secrecy they'd worked so hard to maintain. "As to who in the hospital signed it, I don't remember. Some administrator or doctor."

Harper forced herself to meet his gaze. "The mistakes I made are like neon signs, in hindsight. I wish I'd done things differently." If she'd been open about the pregnancy, would Gage have heard about the baby, or seen his picture in news reports, and realized Shane was his son? Things might have been so different. If only.

"You were young, under a lot of stress, doing the best you could. Don't second-guess yourself now."

She nodded her thanks even though she didn't agree with him. She'd made such foolish decisions. "Anyway, at the time, I had no reason to suspect that she'd lied to me. Or that someone else had lied to her. We were like sisters, really close. I'm more inclined to believe that she wasn't in on the plot and that something bad happened to her."

"At the time of Shane's birth? Or recently?"

She blinked. "Good question. I guess I was thinking that someone stole Shane from her and…did something to her when he was a baby. But if she's the one who stole him, then maybe she's Sam. Or working with Sam."

"Or Sam took Shane from her later, after finding out

whose child he was, thinking he could profit from that knowledge. Do you still have the death certificate?"

Her stomach twisted at the thought of Colette being hurt, or worse, by Sam. In spite of logic telling her Colette had likely been part of the kidnapping scheme all along, she couldn't quite picture the woman she'd thought of as her friend doing something so...insidious. "It's in the safe, near the bottom, with gold leaf around the edge."

He knelt by the safe, sorted through it, and took a picture of the certificate. Then he sent another text, probably to the legion of Seekers working the case. It dawned on her that she couldn't have chosen a more qualified man to help her. Shane had lucked out in the father department. She just hoped her son—their son—got a chance to know the Gage Bishop she'd gotten to know, before everything had gone so wrong between them.

"I need the combination to your safe."

"Should I bother asking why?" She went ahead and told him the combination, which he promptly typed into his phone.

"A Seeker's already on the way here to courier everything to the lab Mason hired. We'll be gone before he arrives."

She stared at him, a bad feeling starting in the pit of her stomach. "Why won't we be here when the courier gets here?"

"Because I'm taking you with me to my home in Gatlinburg. My alarm system is state-of-the-art and my locks will actually keep bad guys out."

She stiffened. "Um, no, *you're* not taking me to Gatlinburg. I can hitch a ride with the courier."

"No. You can't. The lab is in the opposite direction. It would set back the lab tests by hours. Don't worry. I'll give you time to pack a bag before we leave. And we'll have someone keep an eye on your mail and notify us the minute the kidnapper sends another note."

"Stop ignoring the elephant in the room. You're talking about taking me with you...in a *canoe*. That's not happening."

He slid his phone into his pocket. "I've sent the recording of our conversation." He tossed the lab report and evidence bags into the safe and shut the lid before flipping the rug over the top. "You can go ahead and pack a bag to last you for the next couple of days."

"Gage, I'm not stepping foot in a canoe."

He sighed heavily. "You're still afraid of the water, aren't you?"

"Yes. I am. Nearly drowning as a child will do that. I'm terrified of water. You know that. Why would you even think I'd step foot near the creek? I never go back there."

"It wasn't my first plan. I'd assumed I'd stay here with you until the next ransom note showed up. But I had no idea your security was such a disaster." He held up his hands to stop her argument. "I get it. You win. I'll ask another Seeker to drive us both to my house. I can retrieve my car later. Will that work?"

She smiled with relief. "Yes. Thank you."

"No problem. I'll set everything up. You can go ahead and pack and—" His phone buzzed in his pocket. He pulled it out, looked at the screen and swore. "We have to get out of here. Now."

"What? You mean in the canoe? No. I told you. I won't do that. I *can't*."

He took her hand and hauled her to her feet. "I set up some perimeter alarms around your property when I got here. One of them just went off." His fingers fairly flew over the phone as he typed yet another text.

"It must be Blake, my neighbor. He mentioned coming back later, even though I told him not to. He—"

Gage turned the phone around. "Does Blake usually wear camouflage and walk through the woods carrying an M-16 rifle?"

She stared at the screen in horror.

"I didn't think so." He grabbed her hand. "Let's go."

Chapter Eleven

Bishop snatched one of the life vests from the bottom of the canoe and turned around to put it on Harper. She wasn't there. She was twenty feet away, moving at a fast clip through the woods back toward her house.

He swore and threw the vest in the canoe before taking off after her. When he reached her, he used his body to block her way. "Harper, we have to—"

"I can't," she whispered harshly. "Don't you get it? I've tried everything to overcome my fear of water. Nothing works. I would rather face that gunman with my bare hands than get into that stupid canoe. Why can't we just take my car and drive out of here?"

"Keep your voice down," he reminded her. "We *can't* take your car. The gunmen triggered alarms I'd set on your neighbor's property, which gave us the head start we needed to get out before they saw us. But I'm sure they've reached your house by now. Even if we managed to sneak around them without being seen, the moment we start the engine, they'll be on top of us. I'm wicked accurate with a pistol. But I can't out-shoot an M-16."

Her eyes widened as his words sank in. "Gun*men*? Plural? Just how many did those cameras of yours pick up?"

His jaw tightened. "Five."

"Oh my God. What do they want? This doesn't make sense. They can't get their ransom if they kill me."

"This may not be about ransom. It could be a domestic terrorist group out to attack the former president's family, likely in league with the would-be assassin who tried to kill your father this morning. All I know for sure is that people sneaking around in camo with ski masks covering their faces and military-style rifles aren't interested in a civilized chat. I'm sorry to do this, Harper. I really am. But I don't have a choice." He grabbed her, tossed her on his shoulder and took off toward the creek.

Knowing time wasn't on their side, he didn't bother with the life jackets. After peeling Harper's hands from around his neck, he set her in the front of the canoe, the part that was already floating on the water rather than sitting on the bank. It did the job. It kept her from trying to hop out. But the heated glare she gave him as she gripped the sides of the canoe wasn't something he'd likely recover from any time soon.

He shoved the canoe fully into the water and hopped into the back. Using every ounce of his strength, he quickly paddled them into the middle of the creek to take advantage of the strong current. They had to get around that first curve and out of sight before the gunmen figured out where they'd gone. Every muscle in his body was tense, fully expecting a bullet to come slicing through him at any moment. But they rounded the curve without incident, allowing him to breathe a little easier. He set the paddle down and tore off his suit jacket so he could move his arms more freely. Then he grabbed one of the life jackets. "Harper?"

Her back was ramrod-straight, her arms shaking as she clung to both sides of the canoe.

"Harper, here." He pitched the jacket. It landed right behind her. "All you have to do is reach down and grab the life jacket. Put your arms through it, with the opening to the front. Click the buckles together and—"

"No." Her voice sounded strained. If anything, her death grip on the canoe tightened, as evidenced by the mottled look of her hands.

"I'm not even paddling right now. The canoe is floating with the current. I'll keep it nice and steady, okay? Just pick up the jacket and put it on." When she didn't say anything, he added, "I know you're scared. But if you put the vest on, you won't have to be afraid anymore."

"I thought your car was on the other side. Why are we in the middle of the river, parallel with the shoreline instead of heading straight for it?"

"We're still in the creek, not the river. The car's a little ways down. The road didn't quite reach your place."

"How far?" she snapped.

"Not far," he lied, and started paddling again.

His phone buzzed in his pocket. He yanked it out. When he saw Brielle's number on the screen, a feeling of dread shot through him. She knew he was trying to get Harper to safety. He'd texted her while shepherding Harper across her backyard and into the woods. She wouldn't call him unless there was a problem.

He put the phone in speaker mode and shoved it in his shirt pocket so he could talk and still paddle. "What's the sit rep? And keep your voice low." He didn't want Harper hearing something that might make her even more terrified.

"Where are you?" Brielle's voice was barely above a whisper.

Since his phone was encrypted with every bell and whistle Mason's money could buy, he didn't worry about someone intercepting the signal and hearing the conversation, so he spoke plainly, without using code words. "Just past the first bend in the creek. What's your ETA?"

"Dalton and I are already on the property. They were in and out of the house in under a minute. I only know that because of the cameras you set up. We haven't found an obvious trail yet."

"Five guys wearing military-style boots. There have to be some prints in the yard."

"There are, mostly partials, and not that many. They're keeping to harder ground, leaving as few prints as possible. These guys are really good. If I hadn't seen the video from your perimeter alarms, and the cameras you put in the house, I'd swear you were wrong about them even being here. There're no cars, no motorcycles, no four-wheelers. A group of heavily armed men in the middle of nowhere, with no obvious transportation. What's that tell you, Bishop?"

"They've got a boat. They came up the same way I did."

"That's our assumption. Dalton's hoofing it to the creek right now to see if he can spot them anywhere. I'm not far behind. Dang his long legs."

Gage eyed the woods, looking for signs of pursuit. Even though the current was strong, working with his strokes to move them forward, a sense of impending doom settled over him just as it had this morning when he'd followed the suspicious man through the crowd.

The canoe rounded another wide bend, the shore on each side slipping farther away. "We're getting close to the French Broad River. My car's not that much farther after that. Maybe you and Dalton should head back to the house. I don't like the odds if they stumble across you two alone out there."

"Don't worry. We've got the element of surprise. And no way are we leaving your six until we find these guys. Backup is on the way. Caleb and the new Seeker that Mason just hired, Eli Dupree, are bookin' it down the highway, not far behind us. You keep heading to the rendezvous point while we handle things from this end."

"Roger that. I'll call once we're on the road." He ended the call and kept paddling. His deep, long strokes pushed them quickly through the water, but also rocked the canoe from side to side.

Harper definitely noticed.

She was hunched down now, as if trying to lower her center of gravity out of fear that she was going to be tossed from the canoe.

"What's going on?" she called back to him without turning around. "You're paddling like you're trying to win an Olympic race."

He debated what to tell her. He didn't want to make her even more afraid.

"Bishop? Please. I may be terrified but I still want to know what's happening."

Her calling him Bishop again was like a punch in the gut. She'd always called him Gage. Always. The first day he'd introduced himself to her and told her everyone called him Bishop, she'd taken his hand in hers and said she never would. She liked the name Gage. And given she fully intended them to be friends, she wasn't about to call him by his last name. Since that moment, it had become a symbol of their bond and the deep friendship they'd eventually formed.

"Bishop?"

He winced. "Brielle and Dalton are trying to find the gunmen. Caleb and Eli will be at your house soon to help."

"Trying? They don't know where they are?"

"They'll find them. Don't worry."

She was silent for a long moment. "What's this rendezvous point you mentioned? Is it the campground where you parked your car?"

"You heard me say that?"

"Yes. What's the rendezvous point?"

"The campground. It's not much farther. Maybe ten minutes."

"Make it five."

He grinned, relieved that she was talking again, even if it was to give him orders. He maneuvered the canoe around a massive tree dipping down into the water, its roots sticking up like a giant land octopus waiting to snare anyone who got too close.

His phone buzzed, indicating a text coming through. He quickly checked the screen then clenched his jaw to keep a litany of curse words from tumbling out. It was from Caleb. He and Eli had checked Carter's place next door, in case any gunmen were hiding there. He hadn't found any gunmen. But they'd definitely been there.

Blake Carter was dead.

"Bishop? Is something else wrong?"

"You heard the phone buzz in my pocket?"

"Yes. Who was it?"

"You have superhuman hearing. It was Caleb, letting me know that he and Eli arrived to back up Dalton and Brielle." He kept his voice as light as possible, not wanting to alarm her any more than she already was. Carter's murder confirmed beyond a doubt that these men meant business. They were eliminating potential witnesses. It appeared even less likely that their presence could be related to the kidnapper.

The kind of men after them sounded like mercenaries, hired out to the highest bidder. Men like that had no morals, scruples, or loyalties other than to the almighty dollar. Two million dollars was a heck of a lot of money, but not if it was split between the kidnapper and five gunmen. Three-hundred, thirty-thousand a piece, give or take, was hardly enough incentive to justify risking the wrath of the federal government by killing a former president's daughter. Either the ransom was a diversion and not at all the goal, or the mercenaries were working for someone else entirely for a completely different reason.

Was it possible that a kidnapper was trying to ransom Shane at the same time that someone else was trying to kill both the former president and Harper? It seemed so unlikely as to defy belief. So what the heck was going on?

"Bishop."

The new level of panic in her tone had him hyperalert. "What is it?"

"That noise. Do you hear it?"

He stopped paddling, letting the canoe drift as he tuned in to the sounds around them. The drip, drip of water off the paddle onto the surface of the creek. A bird of prey's throaty call as it searched for a late lunch. A rhythmic gritty noise off in the distance. Something man-made.

An engine.

He jerked around. Far off on the horizon, just rounding a curve in the creek, was a small silver boat. It was coming up fast, heading directly for them. The men in the boat wore matching camo. Each one held a rifle.

Gage swore and steered the canoe toward shore. He glanced back. A man in the front of the silver boat raised his rifle and looked through the scope. Bishop scrambled forward, grabbing Harper around the waist.

Her eyes widened with terror as she made a desperate grab for the canoe. "Don't, Bishop! No!"

A bullet pinged through the metal side, barely missing her.

"Take a deep breath, Harper! Hold your breath!"

She screamed as he yanked her over the side and into the water.

Chapter Twelve

Harper screamed in terror as the water closed over her head. She instinctively tried to gulp in air but Bishop's hand clamped down hard over her mouth. His fingers pinched her nose shut as he pulled her deeper into the murky void.

Her lungs burned. Dark spots clouded her vision. She twisted and kicked and fought his hold. She clawed and scratched at his hand on her face. But he held on with a grip so powerful she couldn't break it. Her body jerked back and forth as he kicked the water, propelling them forward with her locked in his deadly embrace.

Bubbles created by the force of his kicks and her flailing limbs rose to the surface, tangling with the long strands of her hair that reached for the blue sky barely visible above them. She tried to lift her hands again to push him away, but she no longer had the energy. Her lungs didn't even burn anymore. A strange calm settled over her. She stopped fighting. Her eyes drifted closed.

Bishop lunged out of the water, gasping for breath as he sprinted into the cover of the trees with Harper's limp body draped over his shoulder. As soon as they were out of sight of the boat circling on the water, searching for them, he dropped to his knees behind a fallen log and laid Harper out on the ground. He knew she hadn't gotten any water in her lungs. He'd kept his hands over her mouth and nose. But she wasn't breathing. She was as limp as a rag doll.

He frantically checked for a pulse. Nothing. He'd held her under too long, desperately trying to shield her from the bullets pinging into the water all around them as he'd kicked toward shore. She hadn't taken a deep breath of air as he had when he'd pulled her over the side of the canoe.

He started CPR, performing chest compressions, desperately trying to start her heart again. "Come on, Harper," he urged. "Come on. Fight."

A shout sounded behind him. He jerked up his head, glancing back toward the water as he kept doing compressions. Sunlight glinted off the silver boat. It was crawling through the water, just past the shoreline as the men on board peered into the underbrush.

He ducked down, trying to stay hidden behind the log as he continued to pump Harper's heart. He couldn't stop now or she wouldn't have any chance at all. And yet, if the gunmen found them here, they'd kill her for sure.

He blew several quick breaths into her lungs then felt for a pulse. Nothing. *God help her. Please.* More compressions. More shouts. He glanced over the top of the log. They were tying the boat to a tree less than thirty yards away. The leader motioned to the others, barking instructions.

"Fight, Harper," he urged next to her ear as he

pushed against her chest. "Fight. Fight for Shane. *Fight for me.* Come on. Breathe."

He glanced over the top of the log again. The boat was secured. Two men were heading away from them, guns drawn as they searched the woods. Two more were headed in their general direction. He didn't see the fifth man anywhere.

They'd be on them soon. It was now or never. He slammed his fist down over her heart as he'd seen someone do on a TV show once. She gasped, her eyes flying open.

Yes! He knew he was probably grinning like a fool.

She blinked up at him in bewilderment. Then a look of pain flashed in her eyes. She moaned and started coughing.

He clamped a hand over her mouth then immediately snatched back his hand. He couldn't do that again. The very idea of cutting off her air had him nauseated. He rose, looking for the men. They weren't there.

"Bish—"

He turned back, pressing his finger against his lips, signaling her to be quiet. He wanted to pull her into his arms, to reassure her, to hold her tight and thank God she was alive. But he couldn't. He had to keep it together. They weren't out of danger by any stretch.

She slowly nodded, letting him know she understood, even as she pressed her hand against her chest and winced.

Guilt rode him. Hard. He'd done that to her, bruised her, possibly cracked some ribs. But he couldn't dwell on that right now. He had to focus. Figure out a way for one man with a pistol to defeat five men with assault rifles. Not exactly encouraging odds.

Glancing around, he pulled his gun from the holster. Still nothing, but that didn't mean the men weren't close by. He looked down at Harper and held up five fingers, then he pointed two fingers to their right, and two to their left. She held up one finger in question, obviously wondering where the fifth gunman was. He shrugged.

She looked past his shoulder, her eyes widening in alarm.

He whirled around, firing his pistol in that direction. The man behind him was dead before he even dropped to the ground.

Shouts sounded from either side of them. Bishop grabbed the dead man's rifle. He threaded the strap over his shoulder and shoved his pistol into his holster. He lifted Harper and threw her onto his back, then took off running toward the only place there didn't seem to be anyone crashing through the woods after them.

The creek.

When he reached the silver boat, he set Harper down and yanked out his knife. He cut the line tying the boat to a tree. Harper started to back away, staring at the water. He braced himself against the censure in her eyes and grabbed her, then lifted her over the side, shoving her down to shield her from sight. Then he hopped in and started the engine.

More shouts sounded from the trees. A bullet pinged into the water not far from the boat. Gage spun the wheel, bringing the boat around. Throttling up, he sent it racing toward the next bend in the river. Another bullet zinged past him, so close he could feel the puff of air beside his head.

He brought the rifle up and laid a line of fire into

the woods even though he couldn't see any of the men. A guttural scream let him know he'd hit at least one of his targets. He turned around to see a tree hanging out of the water directly in front of them. Slamming the throttle back, he jerked the wheel, narrowly avoiding a collision.

"Bishop!"

He felt a tug against his side as he whirled around. Harper had snatched his pistol out of his holster and fired off two rounds toward a couple of men shooting at them from shore. He brought up the rifle and peppered the pair with gunfire. One of them fell forward, his body splashing into the water, floating facedown as the creek turned red around him.

"Go, go, go!" This time it was Harper yelling as she pulled the pistol's trigger over and over, making the men duck for cover.

He opened the throttle all the way and sent the boat speeding in the direction of the mouth of the French Broad River. They'd just rounded the second curve past where the gunmen had attacked them when the engine coughed, sputtered and died.

Immediately the boat began to drift toward shore. Unfortunately, it wasn't the side of the river where they needed to be.

Harper scrambled to him, clinging to seatbacks and railings so she wouldn't lose her balance. "Why did you turn it off?"

"I didn't." He tried to start the engine. Nothing happened. He rushed past her, rocking the small boat as he bent over the end to take a look. An oily smear on the water told him the story even before he saw the bullet hole.

"What is it? What's wrong?" She surprised him by joining him at the back of the boat. She was clutching the side but wasn't practically catatonic like she'd been in the canoe. She looked down at the water then surprised him yet again with some colorful curse words.

"My thoughts exactly." He rushed to the front and looked at the fancy equipment on the console. The engine might be dead but the equipment ran on battery power. He could see the coordinates of where they were in relation to the rendezvous point. Not far. Much closer if they could have used the boat. But they still might have a chance.

The boat was still drifting toward shore but it was moving far too slowly. If they waited for it to get there on its own, the gunmen would catch up to them before then. He glanced at Harper, who was holding on to one of the seats by the railing.

"Harper, there are still three gunmen left. You can bet they're booking it through the woods right now to catch up to us. And they will, if we stay on the boat. We're sitting ducks out here."

Her eyes widened. Then she shook her head. "No. I almost died! You can't ask me to go into the water again." She rubbed her chest as if it still hurt.

He steeled himself against the sympathy and guilt that nearly swamped him. "This time you'll have a life vest on and I'll tow you ashore. I can probably get us there in less than a minute and your head will never be under water."

Great plan. Too bad there weren't any life vests on board. He checked every single possible hiding place, with her watching him the whole time, her face turning paler every time he opened a storage bin and found it empty.

Finally, he sighed and took the pistol from her to secure it in his holster. After strapping the rifle over his shoulder, he held out his hand. "We don't have a choice. We have to get in the water, vest or no vest. Come on."

She held her hands out in front of her as if to stop him and backed up. "I'll take my chances on the boat."

"It's not like last time. I won't throw you in. I'll get in the water first. Just climb over the side, hold on to my back and I'll swim us both to shore."

"I told you no." Her bottom lip trembled. "I can't." She kept backing up, closer to the end of the boat.

He drew a sharp breath. "Harper, wait, you're going to—"

Her legs slammed against the end of the boat. She screamed as she toppled into the water.

"Fall." He hopped over the side after her.

Chapter Thirteen

Harper clung to Bishop's shoulders, floating on top of the water as he swam both of them toward the shore. He probably had bruises from how hard she was holding on. Goodness knows the awful, deep scratches on his hands were likely from her. But she was too scared to let go. The memory of her recent near-death experience was too fresh for her to risk that again.

At least the second time she'd gone into the creek, she'd only been under for a few seconds. Bishop had grabbed her and pulled her head up before she'd swallowed too much of the awful brackish water. As soon as he'd made sure she was okay, he'd placed her hands on his shoulders and carefully turned toward shore and began his powerful strokes.

She couldn't even be mad at him this time. It was her fault she'd fallen in. And, honestly, she couldn't really hold a grudge about the first time, either. He was doing everything he could to protect her. And in calmer moments, when not overcome with fear, she could admit to herself that what he'd done had been—as he'd said—the only choice. He'd saved her life, several times over. And that was just today.

Forcing herself to loosen her grip enough so that she

wouldn't add more injuries to the ones she'd already caused, she dragged in a steadying breath and studied the trees to their left. There wasn't any sign of the men trying to kill them. But they hadn't seemed like the type of men to give up. No doubt, like Bishop had warned, they were hurrying toward them right now.

Bishop shifted, turning to her and taking her hands in his. She clutched them tightly before realizing they were in the shallows. She forced her feet down until she was standing. The water barely reached her hips. Smiling her thanks, she was careful not to talk or to make any noise that might give away their location.

When they reached the water's edge, he pointed to a group of rocks off to the side. She wasn't sure what he was trying to tell her, until he climbed up on the rocks and pointed at the mud close to her. He didn't want them to leave tracks, showing where they'd come on shore. She nodded and tried to climb up on the rocks. He ended up lifting her and setting her down beside him. He motioned for her to follow him, and they headed into the trees.

Once they were on harder ground, they picked up the pace. She noted he was careful about where he stepped and she was equally careful to follow his movements as much as possible. Gradually, the tension in her shoulders began to ease. They hadn't seen or heard anyone in at least ten minutes. Maybe the gunmen had given up after all.

He suddenly stopped. She would have run into him if he hadn't caught her against his side. Without looking at her, he stared at a stand of trees to their left. But there wasn't anything out of the ordinary there, not that she saw, at least. He looked to the right, as well, and again she saw nothing to explain his alarm.

But she did *hear* something.

Or rather, she heard *nothing*. Earlier, the sounds of the river had been all around them. The occasional chirp of a bird. Insects buzzing or whizzing past. An animal snuffling around in the bushes. But now? It was as if someone had pressed Pause on a noisy movie and the silence was nearly deafening.

He tugged her along behind him, his steps careful like before but fast, so fast she had to jog to keep up with his long strides. Then he was pulling her behind a hollowed-out oak tree and taking out his pistol. He surprised her by handing it to her and leaning down until his lips were next to her ear.

"From what I saw earlier, you're comfortable with a pistol, right?"

She whispered back, "Yes. Did you see someone?"

"No. But they're close. And we're still outgunned. I need to try to take them out one by one to give us a chance." He pressed her back into the hollowed-out section of the tree. "Can you hide here for me? Just for a few minutes? If you see anyone, shoot. Don't give them a second chance. They wouldn't give you one. Can you do that?"

She swallowed hard and nodded. She wasn't actually sure that she could shoot someone like that. But his urgency told her they were in deep trouble, so she'd have to try. Before she could even blink, he was gone, melting into the forest like a wraith.

Trying not to think about the other creatures and insects that might be sharing the tree with her, she clutched the gun in both hands, wincing when the movement made her chest hurt. Then she settled in to wait.

BISHOP ADJUSTED THE rifle over his shoulder to keep it from bumping against him as he crept through the bushes and trees. The rifle was a last resort. The sound would draw the others right to him. Surprise was his best element of defense right now. And his best weapons were ones that made no sound: his knife and his hands.

Crouching, he studied the ground where he'd seen some bushes move moments earlier. Sure enough, he found a set of boot prints. As Brielle had warned, his prey was careful, leaving only a hint of a trail to follow. But Bishop had done more than his share of tracking before, mostly while hunting with his father and brother. He was able to find a few bent blades of grass that told the story.

Moving to a more defensible position, with trees at his back, he watched, and waited. A few moments later, a whisper of fabric sounded off to his left. He dove to his right, rolling out of the way as a spurt of gunfire peppered the ground. He jerked back behind a tree as another gunman crashed through the brush up ahead, coming to help the first man.

Bishop moved with lightning speed, sprinting around the trees and launching himself at the first gunman. The man's shocked gaze met Bishop's a split second before Bishop violently twisted the man's neck. He slumped dead to the ground and Bishop was off and running before the other man even realized what was happening.

A guttural yell sounded from the second man.

Bishop dove behind a tree as bullets strafed across the ground. The man was shooting indiscriminately, pumping bullets into the woods all around him, yelling his rage and making it easy for Bishop to pinpoint exactly where he was.

Bishop calmly tugged his rifle down from his back and waited behind a thick oak tree. Firing indiscriminately wasn't an option for him. His opponent was wearing body armor. He could shoot his legs to bring him down. But the kill shot had to be a head shot.

As soon as the shooting stopped, he lunged forward and strafed the man's legs with bullets. His body jerked like a marionette on a string as he screamed and fell to the earth. Bishop finished him off with a single, deadly shot, then dove for cover, fully expecting the last gunman to have followed all the noise and try to ambush him.

Several minutes passed in silence. Bishop listened intently, studying the woods around him. Nothing. The gunshots had practically been an invitation. Why wasn't the last gunman there, trying to end this?

Because he didn't care about Bishop. He was going after the main target. Harper.

His stomach dropped. He took off running.

When he reached the towering dead oak with the hollowed-out middle, he ran to the side, sweeping the rifle out in front of him. The gunman wasn't there. Relieved, he whispered, "Harper, it's Bishop. Lower the pistol. I'm going to step in front of the tree."

He lowered his rifle and swung around to face her. The tree was empty. Harper was gone.

He stared incredulously at the hollowed center of the tree. His pulse rushed in his ears. His hand shook as he felt the bark inside, fearing he'd find blood. When his hand came away dry, he let out a relieved breath. The gunman hadn't killed her, at least not here. There was still a chance. But he had to find her. Fast.

"Bishop?"

He whirled around.

Harper stood on the opposite side of the clearing.

Gage jerked his rifle to the side and ran to her, scanning the woods around them as he went. When he reached her, he yanked her behind a tree and then turned her around to face him.

"What happened?" he rasped. "I told you to wait in the protection of the tree."

"I did," she whispered back. "But I heard someone coming through the woods. Then I saw him, on the other side of the clearing, searching the bushes, looking for me."

"You should have shot him."

"He had body armor. I'm not confident enough that I could have…taken a…"

"Head shot?"

She nodded, her complexion turning slightly ashen at his words. "I crept out of the hollow and hid behind a log a little deeper in the woods until he left."

He wanted to drag her against him and never let her go. She was so brave, and smart. He couldn't have been more proud of her. He had to clear his tight throat to be able to talk. "Which way did he go?"

"Upriver. Where we were going until the boat engine was destroyed."

"How long ago did he come through here?"

"Hard to stay. Not long after I heard gunshots sounding from the opposite direction. What happened? Did you find the other men?"

"I found them." He settled his rifle across his shoulder again. "They won't be bothering us anymore."

She wrapped her arms around her middle, looking a bit lost, overwhelmed.

"Let's head back toward your property. The Seekers are there. Let's hope the last gunman keeps going in the other direction." He took her hand to pull her with him. Instead, he pulled her toward him, unable to resist the impulse to hold her.

She wrapped her arms around his waist and buried her face against his chest. He heaved a shaky breath, not sure what he would have done if she'd rejected his touch. After the canoe, her nearly being shot a dozen times at least, then thinking he'd been too late, that the last gunman had gotten to her, he was nearly out of his mind with guilt, worry and grief. Now, just holding her like this, it was like taking the magic elixir. He was calming down, feeling centered, back in control.

"Thank God you're okay," he whispered against the top of her head.

Her hands tightened around him but she didn't say anything.

When he realized they'd been standing there for at least a full minute, he forced himself to release her and step back. He stared down into her tremulous eyes and gently held her upper arms. "When I saw that empty tree hollow, I almost lost it. I thought I'd failed you again. That the gunman had you."

She gave him a sad smile. "You've never failed me, Bishop. Not once. Don't you get that? Nothing that happened in the past was your fault. Did it hurt that you didn't believe me about the pregnancy? Of course. But knowing what I know now, that you don't remember what happened between us that night, how could I expect you to have believed me?"

He took another step back, uncomfortable with her praise. "You should be angry with me, Harper. I don't deserve your forgiveness. I haven't earned it." Before she could argue with him, he took her hand. "Let's go. It's too dangerous to stand here any longer."

Without waiting for her reply, he tugged her along with him toward the river's edge so he could use it as a roadmap back to her property. A few minutes later, a sound downriver had him pulling her into the cover of trees.

"What's wrong?" she murmured. "Is it the gunman?"

He peered around a tree and then smiled his first real smile in a long time. "No. It's the Knights of the Round Table." He pointed downriver toward a small blue boat motoring around a curve, Dalton standing in the prow. There was no mistaking that black Stetson.

"The Justice Seekers are here."

Chapter Fourteen

Bishop looked past Brielle and Dalton, standing on the shore beside him. Harper was already in the boat, sitting on the floor so she was barely visible rather than up on a seat where she'd be too easy a target. Caleb was crouching in front of her, fastening her life jacket, while Eli stood guard, rifle hanging at his waist as he studied the shoreline with a pair of binoculars, searching for potential threats.

Harper wasn't panicking and had gotten onto the boat with surprisingly little fuss. But she was so pale, it was obvious she was scared. Considering the last two times she'd been on the water, he couldn't blame her one bit.

"She'll be okay," Brielle assured him. "Caleb and Eli won't let anything happen to her."

Dalton nodded. "The sooner you show us where the bodies are, the sooner we can mark the GPS coordinates for the cops and get back on the boat."

"Right." Bishop forced himself to turn away from Harper. He pointed to a gap in the trees upriver. "Dalton, dead guys three and four are in that direction. One was lying half in the water just past that next curve in the river, last I saw him. The other one is a good fifty yards in, perpendicular to his location."

"Got it. I'll let you know once I find them." He jogged just inside the tree line then began following the curve of the river in the opposite direction.

"Bad guys one and two are this way." He and Brielle headed into the trees.

Dalton texted Brielle's phone just a few minutes later that he'd found both guys, and tagged the GPS coordinates. It took a bit longer for Bishop and Brielle to find their two. Finally, with all four dead mercenaries accounted for, they headed back to the boat.

Some of the tension eased from Bishop's shoulders when he saw the boat still sitting where they'd left it, Eli and Caleb standing guard while Harper sat cross-legged in the bottom. He smiled at her when he climbed on board and sat on her far side so that he shielded her from the shoreline when the boat turned around and headed back in the direction of her home.

He didn't try to talk to her. He could tell she was struggling to hold back her panic. Instead, he scooted closer until his knees pressed against hers, trying without words to let her know that he was there and would watch over her. She glanced at him in surprise then gifted him with a smile.

Dalton sat beside him, lending his bulk as an additional shield. Brielle had taken up guard duty beside Eli, providing another layer between the shore and Harper while Caleb drove the boat.

Dalton motioned to the mouth of the creek as they left the river and steered into the more narrow waterway. "We'll be there in a few minutes. I've updated

Mason. He's handling the police and contacting former president Manning to let him know what happened."

Harper's head shot up. "Police? We can't involve the police. The kidnapper might see the police and think I called them, that I told them about the ransom." She gave Bishop a pleading look. "He'll…he might hurt Shane."

Her fear was palpable. He wanted to tell her everything would be okay. But he couldn't. Truth was, he wasn't sure. And he was scared, too, worried his son might pay the price for today's fiasco.

"We can't avoid telling the police," he told her. "There are four dead men in the woods. Someone is bound to stumble onto them at some point, either a camper or hunter or just someone out hiking. This isn't something we can ignore or cover up."

He exchanged a knowing glance with Dalton over the top of her head. There weren't just four deaths they had to worry about. There were five. But he hadn't told her about Blake Carter.

If it wasn't for Carter, the Seekers could and probably would have covered up the deaths of the mercenaries. But Carter's death had taken that option away. He wasn't an unknown, unnamed mercenary who no one would go looking for in a public forum. He had a job, presumably a family and friends who would notice his absence. The only way to ensure that none of the Seekers got caught up as suspects in his murder was to level with the police and answer their questions.

Harper looked from him to Dalton and back again. "What about Shane? The police presence will alert the kidnapper."

"It might. But I wouldn't worry just yet. Remember

his incentive. Two million dollars. He's not going to throw that away without being absolutely sure that he has no chance to collect his windfall. When we talk to the police, we won't mention Shane or the ransom."

Dalton had been listening to their conversation with rapt attention. "We've got two completely different bad guys."

"Looks like it," Bishop agreed. He watched the shoreline slide past them. "We're not that far from your property, Harper. We need to get our stories straight."

She stared at him. "No mention of the kidnapper, or Shane. But how do I explain you being at my home? And the Seekers getting involved?"

"That part's easy. The Seekers, including me, were part of your father's security detail for his trip to Gatlinburg. When I stopped the would-be assassin, your father asked for an audience with me, which I granted. From that point, we tweak a few things. You say that we had a private meeting after your father thanked me, so we could catch up on old times."

She slowly nodded. "Makes sense. I can do that. But what about you coming to my house? In a canoe?"

"Yeah, well. That's where we get creative. We capitalize on the truth—that your father and I aren't fans of each other, but without saying why. Just say that we never got along. To explain why I'd sneak onto your property instead of driving right up, we say that I did it so your father wouldn't find out."

She frowned. "And that would explain you coming there in a canoe how?"

Dalton stood. "I think this is my cue to check on Caleb to see if he needs my help docking this thing. We borrowed the boat from the neighbor on the far side of

Carter's property. We'll have to let y'all off at Harper's property, then head down the creek to return the boat. My car's parked there as collateral. We'll drive to Harper's place as soon as we're done."

When he was at the front of the boat with Caleb, Harper gave Bishop a suspicious look. "I have a feeling I'm not going to like this. Otherwise your friend wouldn't have been so quick to escape."

"Yes, well… He knows what I'm about to say. It's a cover story that Mason suggested, one that he's going to tell your father, too, if he hasn't already."

"And what's this cover story?"

He cleared his throat. "That you and I are, uh, attracted to each other. Always have been. And we kind of struck up that attraction in our meeting earlier. We decided to sneak and meet each other today. That explains why I hid when your sister was there, so we can keep the timeline straight."

She blinked a few times then finally said, "That's hardly necessary. Can't you just say I was inviting all of the Seekers to my place to thank them for saving my father? And for some reason you decided to come by canoe? I mean, it's eccentric, but it's closer to the truth."

"You're right. Except for one thing. Our goal isn't just to have a story for the police so we can cover up the ransom angle. It's also to ensure the kidnapper doesn't suspect that I was sneaking onto the property as your protector and that we're all trying to help you. It would be the same as you going to the police or FBI for help. By playing up the save-your-father aspect, as you said, which we'd planned to do already, that provides a reasonable cover for why the Seekers are here.

But me sneaking you out back by canoe puts all of that into question. Playing up the lovers angle makes it more believable to the kidnapper."

She nodded but didn't look pleased with the idea. "You really think all of that works as a story? And explains why the other Seekers are here?"

"Absolutely. As long as you let me do most of the talking, I'll provide answers for all of their questions. Just go along with what I say. I don't like the hand we've been dealt. Me being here at all was supposed to be hush-hush so the kidnapper would never realize you'd asked me to help. But it's going public now, the part about those gunmen. All we can do is try to control how it's spun and hope the kidnapper sees it the same way."

The sound of the engine changed as Caleb slowed the boat. Dalton was pointing at a spit of land that jutted out into the creek at the back of Harper's land. It formed a natural dock of sorts. Caleb nodded and slowed even more, guiding the boat toward the outcrop.

"Don't worry," Bishop said. "I'll be with you the whole time we speak to the police. Just follow my lead." Without waiting for her reply, he got to his feet and joined Brielle a few feet away, still keeping watch. "Brielle, did you get a chance to get those things from the safe?"

She nodded, smiling past him at Harper. "I did. I gathered up all your perimeter alarms and cameras, too. Didn't figure you'd want anyone asking about those. They're hidden in the woods until we can retrieve them."

"Good thinking. Thanks, Brielle."

"Bishop?" Harper called out. "Are you worried the police will search my house?"

"There's no question they'll search it. They'll have to clear it and make sure no one is hiding inside. Ordinarily, we could stall them and demand a warrant. But not in exigent circumstances like this."

"Then there's something else you might want to get out of the house before they go inside." She cleared her throat. "I made a baby book for Shane. It documents my pregnancy and has a page at the back dedicated to the story of what happened to him, including his date of death."

Bishop exchanged a surprised look with Brielle. "Where's the baby book?"

"Under my mattress."

"Brielle—"

"No problem," she assured them. "I'll get the baby book, too. Mason's going to notify the police after he talks to your father, again, to keep our stories consistent. He's also going to make sure we have enough time to get back and take care of any loose ends before making the call to the police. We have time."

Harper gave her a grateful smile. "Thank you. I appreciate everything you're all doing to try to protect Shane."

"We'd do anything for Bishop," Brielle said. "We're a family. And right now, that extends to you and your son. I'll just pop inside and grab that book before the police search the house. No problem."

The boat bumped up against a sapling on the edge of the little peninsula. Dalton leaped across the few feet of water and tied the rope around the sapling, stabilizing it so the others could get off.

Bishop looked toward shore then cursed beneath his breath.

Harper stood, tightly gripping the chair beside her. "What's wrong?"

He said something to Brielle and turned around. "Seems the timing of Mason's call to the police was a little off." He waved a hand toward her property just as a group of four uniformed officers and a man in a suit who was nearly as big as Bishop emerged from the woods. "They're already here."

Harper followed his gaze, her eyes widening in alarm.

"Caleb," Bishop said, keeping his voice low, "looks like you and Dalton will have to return the boat later than planned. I could use your help creating a diversion so Brielle can get in and out of the house without the police realizing what she's doing."

"No worries," Caleb replied.

Bishop bent and lifted Harper in his arms.

She stared at him in shock. "What are you doing?"

"Did you hear me mention a diversion?"

"Picking me up is a diversion?"

He grinned. "It certainly is. But it will be an even better diversion, for the cops, when you faint."

"What?"

"Close your eyes, Harper. Don't open them until I tell you to."

"But I—"

"Do it. Now."

She closed her eyes and went limp in his arms.

He settled her higher against his chest and stepped over the side of the boat onto land.

The group of police officers stopped in front of him.

The one in the suit held up his credentials. "I'm Detective Nick Radley. We're investigating a homicide." His eyes widened. "Is that who I think it is?"

"If you think it's former president Manning's daughter Harper, you're right. She nearly drowned and I had to revive her. I thought she was going to be okay but she just fainted. Call an ambulance." He brushed past them.

"Hey. Wait a minute," the detective called out.

Bishop ignored him and strode into the woods.

Chapter Fifteen

Harper sat in the back of the ambulance in her driveway, being examined by one of the EMTs while the other one sat in the cab. Bishop stood outside the double doors, having an often heated discussion with Detective Radley, who didn't seem the least bit intimidated by Bishop—probably because they were both almost the same height and equally broad-shouldered.

As they verbally sparred, Bishop kept a watchful eye on her. With the EMT asking questions and poking and prodding her, it was difficult for Harper to focus on Bishop's conversation or to hear what they were saying. But she did catch two words, spoken in disgust several times by the detective.

Brielle Walker.

Apparently, she was a former police officer, which made Radley even more livid that she'd disappeared rather than stick around to be interviewed. During the confusion of Bishop carrying Harper inside and laying her on the couch, with Eli, Caleb and Dalton all talking at once, distracting the cops, Brielle had slipped down the hallway. And she'd never come back. Radley had several cops looking for her right now. Harper prayed they didn't find her.

Beyond Bishop and Radley, she could see that the coroner's van was still parked in Blake's driveway, partially obscured by some of the oleander bushes her stepmom had insisted on planting when she'd bought the place. All that Radley would reveal was that a friend of Blake's had stopped by, then called 9-1-1 after discovering his body. Mason hadn't made a mistake and called the police too early after all. They were already on their way when he'd made his call, which just had Radley even more suspicious wondering why the call hadn't come in earlier if they'd left her house to get away from armed gunmen.

Clearly, Blake had been murdered, since that was the homicide Radley was investigating. But why had he been killed? And did it have anything to do with the gunmen who'd gone after her and Bishop? Those were the types of questions on everyone's mind, especially the extremely curious and determined Detective Radley.

Caleb and one of the uniformed policemen stepped past the ambulance and stood on the carport. Caleb gave her a subtle nod, as if to reassure her that everything was okay. Hopefully, that meant Brielle had successfully gotten away. Although how she'd managed it was a complete mystery. The place was swarming with police now. They were in her house, in Blake's house, grid-searching both properties, including the woods out back. And a handful had arrived by boat about forty minutes ago and had taken Dalton and Eli with them to locate the gunmen's bodies.

The sudden burn of tears in her eyes had her wiping her tears before they could fall. She ruthlessly tamped down her emotions. But it wasn't easy. She was so scared, terrified that the kidnapper was watching, that he saw all of this police activity and concluded that she'd broken his rules. She prayed he wouldn't give up on the ransom exchange, that he wouldn't hurt Shane. It was so frustrating not having a way to contact this Sam person, to make sure that her son was okay.

"Ms. Manning?" The EMT looked at her with concern. "Are you in pain?"

She wiped her eyes again. "No. I'm okay." She offered him a watery smile. "Thanks."

He didn't seem convinced. "Those are impressive contusions on your ribs. They're going to turn a rainbow of colors over the next few days." He sat back on the bench across from her. "Your vitals are good. And I didn't feel any breaks. But you could still have a cracked rib or two. It happens sometimes with CPR I'd like to take you to the hospital for some X-rays."

Radley stepped closer to the doorway. "Are those contusions consistent with CPR or could they have been caused by some sort of a struggle?"

The EMT blinked, his eyes widening. "I, uh, I'm not—"

"Knock it off, Radley," Bishop interrupted. "Whatever happened to Blake has nothing to do with Ms. Manning."

Ignoring Bishop, Radley asked, "Was he a love interest? Did you two have a fight and you shot him?"

Harper gasped in shock.

Bishop narrowed his eyes at the detective. "Whatever happened to him isn't Harper's fault, or ours. If he's been shot, as you said, that's consistent with the gunmen who tried to shoot Harper and me. They likely killed him before going after her, to ensure there weren't any witnesses."

"Right." Skepticism practically dripped from Radley's voice. "And why would these armed killers go after her to begin with?"

"I'm sure you heard about the attempted assassination of former president Manning this morning in Gatlinburg. Is it really hard to believe that there may have been a coordinated attempt to go after his daughter, too? I'm sure the Secret Service will be crawling all over this soon. You might want to work on getting real evidence and real leads before then or you'll be left out in the cold. Hint, badgering the victim isn't the way to do that."

"Gentlemen," the EMT said, "I really think we should get Ms. Manning to the hospital. She could have some cracked ribs. And since she ingested brackish water, it's likely she'll need to be put on antibiotics to fight any potential infection."

Harper pressed a hand to her chest and sucked in a breath when she touched one of the deep bruises. "Do you really think my ribs are cracked? It doesn't hurt that much as long as I don't press on them. I mean, I can breathe just fine."

"Didn't you faint earlier? That makes me think you weren't breathing deeply due to the pain and passed out from lack of oxygen."

"Um, yes. Or maybe I was just overwrought."

He gave her a doubtful look. "Take a deep breath."

She tried, but gasped at the sharp pain.

Bishop stepped closer to the back of the ambulance. "That's it. You're going to the hospital."

"I really don't think that's necessary. And I want

YOU pick your books –
WE pay for everything.
You get up to FOUR New Books and TWO Mystery Gifts...absolutely FREE

Dear Reader,

I am writing to announce the launch of a huge **FREE BOOKS GIVEAWAY**... and to let you know that YOU are entitled to choose up to FOUR fantastic books that WE pay for.

Try **Harlequin® Romantic Suspense** books featuring heart-racing page-turners with unexpected plot twists and irresistible chemistry that will keep you guessing to the very end.

Try **Harlequin Intrigue® Larger-Print** books featuring action-packed stories that will keep you on the edge of your seat. Solve the crime and deliver justice at all costs. family and community unite.

Or TRY BOTH!

In return, we ask just one favor: Would you please participate in our brief Reader Survey? We'd love to hear from you.

This FREE BOOKS GIVEAWAY means that we pay for everything! We'll even cover the shipping, and no purchase is necessary, now or later. So please return your survey today.

You'll get **Two Free Books** and **Two Mystery Gifts** from each series to try, altogether worth over **$20!**

Sincerely

Pam Powers

Pam Powers
For Harlequin Reader Service

Complete the survey below and return it today to receive up to 4 FREE BOOKS and FREE GIFTS guaranteed!

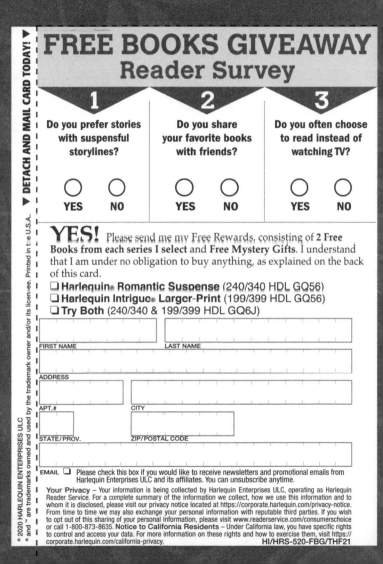

▼ DETACH AND MAIL CARD TODAY! ▼

FREE BOOKS GIVEAWAY
Reader Survey

1

Do you prefer stories with suspenseful storylines?

◯ YES   ◯ NO

2

Do you share your favorite books with friends?

◯ YES   ◯ NO

3

Do you often choose to read instead of watching TV?

◯ YES   ◯ NO

YES! Please send me my Free Rewards, consisting of **2 Free Books from each series I select** and **Free Mystery Gifts**. I understand that I am under no obligation to buy anything, as explained on the back of this card.

☐ Harlequin® Romantic Suspense (240/340 HDL GQ56)
☐ Harlequin Intrigue® Larger-Print (199/399 HDL GQ56)
☐ Try Both (240/340 & 199/399 HDL GQ6J)

FIRST NAME

LAST NAME

ADDRESS

APT.#

CITY

STATE/PROV.

ZIP/POSTAL CODE

EMAIL ☐ Please check this box if you would like to receive newsletters and promotional emails from Harlequin Enterprises ULC and its affiliates. You can unsubscribe anytime.

Your Privacy – Your information is being collected by Harlequin Enterprises ULC, operating as Harlequin Reader Service. For a complete summary of the information we collect, how we use this information and to whom it is disclosed, please visit our privacy notice located at https://corporate.harlequin.com/privacy-notice. From time to time we may also exchange your personal information with reputable third parties. If you wish to opt out of this sharing of your personal information, please visit www.readerservice.com/consumerschoice or call 1-800-873-8635. **Notice to California Residents** – Under California law, you have specific rights to control and access your data. For more information on these rights and how to exercise them, visit https://corporate.harlequin.com/california-privacy.

HI/HRS-520-FBG/THF21

® 2020 HARLEQUIN ENTERPRISES ULC

® and ™ are trademarks owned and used by the trademark owner and/or its licensee. Printed in the U.S.A.

to know what's going on. Have they caught the last gunman?"

"Good question. Radley, we gave you the GPS coordinates of the four bodies and Dalton and Eli took your guys upriver to show them in person. What's going on there now?"

"I received a text a little while ago that the bodies have been found. But there's no indication there was a fifth man. Are you sure you counted right?"

Bishop shot the detective a look that should have incinerated him. "We're done here." He hopped inside the back of the ambulance.

The EMT's brows shot up to his hairline but he scooted over to make room beside him.

"Let the driver know we're ready to go to the hospital. I want to make sure Ms. Manning gets those antibiotics on board and has her ribs x-rayed." Bishop leaned out and pulled the left door shut. But before he could shut the right door, the detective grabbed it.

"I'm not through asking questions," Radley said.

Bishop looked pointedly at the detective's hand. "Talk to Caleb. He's on the carport being interviewed by one of your officers. I'm going to close the other door. Whether you move your hand or not is up to you. We're taking Ms. Manning to the hospital right now." He shoved the detective's hand off the door.

Radley hopped up into the ambulance, standing in the tight space between Bishop's knees and the gurney where Harper was sitting. "I certainly wouldn't want to interfere with her care. I'll just ask my questions on the way to the hospital." He slammed the door closed.

Bishop leaned forward as if to toss Radley onto the gravel driveway.

Harper quickly slid over to the far end of the gurney and patted the space beside her. "Detective, won't you sit down?" She hadn't missed that Radley's right hand was hovering near his holstered gun.

Bishop's jaw tightened. "Harper, you don't have to put up with this. I can get rid of him."

Radley snorted.

Bishop started to rise.

Harper leaned over and grabbed his arm. "It's okay. *Please.* I don't mind answering his questions." She smiled at the EMT, who looked like *he* was about to faint.

After a long minute, Bishop finally gave her a crisp nod. "All right. But if he's a jerk to you, I'm throwing him onto the highway."

Instead of seeming angry, Radley looked amused, which had Bishop looking ready to kill him.

Harper rushed to prevent imminent bloodshed. "Let's go," she urged the EMT.

He nodded enthusiastically and rapped on the wall of the cab, signaling the driver.

Chapter Sixteen

Harper felt sorry for the EMT. He'd scrunched himself into the corner, as far from the other two men as
he could get. She couldn't blame him. She didn't want
to be there, either. And since she was obviously sta-
ble and this wasn't an emergency, they were running
lights only, no sirens, and appeared to be doing the
speed limit. That meant this was going to be a long,
uncomfortable ride for all of them. And not just because it was so tight inside the back of a vehicle that
didn't seem designed to hold more than two people.

The tension was palpable as the detective pulled out
his phone. "I'm going to record our conversation so I
don't forget anything."

"No." Bishop crossed his arms.

Radley gave him a disgusted look. "What's the problem now?"

"I don't trust you."

"I don't trust you, either. That is exactly why recording our conversation provides both of us with protection, proof of what was said or not said, if we need it
later."

Bishop shook his head. "The point is that I don't
trust you not to try to capitalize on the fact that you're

interviewing the daughter of the former president of the United States."

"What? Oh good grief. You think I'm going to sell the recording to some gossip rag and try to make money off it?"

"It wouldn't be the first time someone's done that. Would it, Harper?"

She sighed. "No. It wouldn't. There were a few enterprising jerks in college who snapped pictures of me or recorded my private conversations and sold them."

The detective snorted. "I'm not some college kid trying to make a fast buck. But, fine. We'll do this the old-fashioned way." He put his phone away and pulled out a small notebook and pen. "Is this acceptable, Bishop?"

"Of course it is. Don't be an ass."

Harper stared at him in alarm. *"Bishop."*

The detective surprised her by smiling. "It's okay." He slid the pen and notebook back into his suit jacket. "How about we take this down a couple of notches. No recordings, no notes. No one's under arrest—"

"No kidding," Bishop said. "Since Ms. Manning is the victim here."

"That may prove to be true. But take a minute to look at this from my point of view. I got a call from Dispatch to check out a murder scene. When I arrived, the scene had been secured, but there are a few remarkably hard-to-find shoe prints indicating the murderer went next door, to Ms. Manning's home.

"We manage to find a few more prints leading into the woods. So we head that way, guns out because we're expecting the murderer might be hiding close by. Once we arrive at the creek, we see a boat approaching with a woman sitting on the floor of that boat surrounded by heavily armed people. Then we're told five other armed men are the bad guys and tried to kill the woman, but that four of them have been killed and one is still on the loose." He held his hands out to his sides. "Can you see how it's just a tad confusing from my perspective? A bit hard to separate out the good guys and bad guys and what's really going on? Wouldn't you be suspicious if you were in my shoes?"

Harper exchanged a long look with Bishop. His mouth quirked before he surprised her by holding out his hand toward Radley. "My apologies, Detective. My concern for Ms. Manning has me a little cranky."

Radley's brows arched, but he readily shook Bishop's hand. "A *little* cranky?"

"Don't push it."

Radley grinned. "So noted. Let's back up and start with some basics. Maybe you can both help me pin down a time of death window for Mr. Carter. Ms. Manning, when's the last time you saw him?"

"Earlier today."

"What time was that? What were the circumstances?"

"I was in Gatlinburg this morning, to meet with my dad. There was the attempted shooting of my father—"

"That your former Secret Service agent foiled." He glanced at Bishop. "Your face is all over the news along with a little backstory. I recognized you the moment I saw you on that boat, which is the only reason we didn't come out of the woods shooting. And it's why I asked the uniforms not to arrest all of you while we sorted this thing out."

"The media actually helped for a change," Bishop said. "Guess there's a first time for everything."

Radley smiled. "You were saying, Ms. Manning?"

"I, uh, yes. Well, I met with my dad probably an hour after the attempted assassination."

"Close to ten o'clock then, if reports about the shooting were accurate."

"That sounds right. I met with Dad, then Bishop, then went straight home."

"What did you meet about?"

"What's that got to do with anything?" Bishop asked.

Radley shrugged. "Maybe nothing. Maybe everything. My job is to gather as much information as I can until I can form a picture that will help me figure out what's going on. Is there a reason you don't want Ms. Manning to tell me about those meetings?"

Bishop glanced at her. She realized this was it, where the lies had to start, so they could keep the ransom demand a secret. Time to become the actress she'd never wanted to be.

She gave him a shaky smile. "It's okay… *Gage*. He's not the paparazzi. And he's not recording anything."

Gage subtly nodded as if to reassure her. Then he motioned to the EMT. "Detective Radley might not be who we need to worry about."

The EMT's eyes widened and his face reddened like a child caught eavesdropping outside someone's door.

Two minutes later, they were back on the road, heading for Knoxville, both EMTs now in the cab.

"No more evasive answers," Radley said. "Unless the meeting was some kind of state secret—which doesn't make sense since Mr. Manning is the former president, not the current one—there's no reason you can't tell me what the meeting was about."

"It was just a photo op, a meeting with the press so my father could publicly thank Gage for saving his life."

"Then why the secrecy?"

"Because the meeting didn't turn out as planned. Gage doesn't have a great history with my father. They don't like each other. At all. Gage refused the photo op and wouldn't allow my father to thank him in front of reporters. Instead, my father and the others stepped out of the room so that Gage and I could meet for a few minutes."

The detective didn't seem surprised by her declaration, probably because she was making a point of using Bishop's first name, as someone intimately involved with him would. Now that she was calling him Gage again as part of the act for Radley, it felt as natural as breathing. It felt...right slipping into that old familiarity. He'd always been Gage to her. It was something special the two of them had shared. Calling him Bishop earlier today had been childish, her way of getting back at him because he'd made her mad. She wasn't proud of how she'd handled the stress and lashed out.

"What was discussed in the private meeting between you two?" Radley prodded.

Harper didn't have to work at looking uncomfortable. Her emotions from that meeting were still too raw. And she was afraid she might say something that could jeopardize Shane. She looked up at Gage, silently pleading for him to take over.

"It's okay," he told her. "Detective, as you've no doubt surmised, Harper and I have a...history. We didn't part on good terms and haven't seen each other in years. But when we saw each other this morning...

well, we realized the attraction we'd always had was still there. She told her dad she wanted to thank me for saving his life and since I refused to even discuss it with the media present, he allowed us to have a private audience. We decided then and there that we wanted to see each other again."

"Romantically."

Harper's face heated.

"Yes," Gage said. "But her father doesn't approve of me, so we—"

"He doesn't approve of you because—what?—when you were the Secret Service agent protecting his daughter, you two hooked up?"

Harper gasped in surprise. "That's not what—"

"Yes," Gage said. "We were lovers, a very long time ago. That's why her father hates me."

Harper stared at him, stunned.

"And why you were fired as a Secret Service agent, I'm guessing?"

"I didn't know that was common knowledge. But, yes. You're correct."

Harper clutched her hands together to keep from reaching out to him. She hated that a man so honorable had to admit to being fired, for something that she didn't feel was his fault. His pride had to be hurting. And she wished she could somehow take away that hurt.

"Interesting. Go on. You were explaining, I think, that you and Ms. Manning were planning to see each other again."

Gage gave him a terse nod. "We came up with a plan for her to have a get-together for all of the Justice Seekers at her place to thank them for providing additional security at today's event." He hesitated. "I assume one of the others already explained about our company?"

Radley tapped his fingers against the gurney. "I know enough to fill up a few sentences in my notebook. But I'll work on fleshing that out later. You and your coworkers went to Ms. Manning's home and you were there when she saw her neighbor?"

"No." Harper cleared her throat. "I got home close to noon. I, uh, was hoping to spruce up the house before the Seekers arrived. But before I could get in the door, Blake came over." She explained about the brief visit, and then about her sister already being there with her boyfriend.

"Cynthia? Your middle sibling?"

"Yes."

"And you have a much younger brother, too, if I recall correctly?"

"Tyler. He's eleven."

Radley pulled out his notebook and pen, then hesitated. "Is it okay if I write some of this down? I'm going to mix it all up if I don't."

"It's fine," she said.

"Okay, let's see. I'm trying to keep the family dynamics straight. If I remember right, your mother died when you were little, then your father married his current wife?"

"How is this relevant?" Gage asked.

"Puzzle pieces. You never know which one you're missing."

"It's okay," she assured both of them. "I've been asked about my family a million times. Everyone seems to have trouble keeping it straight. My mom, Hope, died of breast cancer when I was nine. Dad had a really hard time moving on, so he went to group therapy. That's where he met Julia. She'd just lost her spouse, too. A couple of years later, they—my dad and Julia—got married. Cynthia was Julia's daughter from a previous marriage. But Tyler is both of theirs."

"Wait, okay. So Cynthia's not blood related to you? She's your stepsister? But Tyler's father is your dad, Earl Manning. So he's your half brother?"

"They're both my siblings. Blood-related or not."

He glanced up from the notes he was taking. "No offense intended. Again, I don't know that any of this matters. But if it does, I don't want to get it wrong. Sometimes there are issues in families, like jealousy, that might be important to know. You did say your sister Cynthia—no blood relation—broke into your home and was waiting for you. And not long after that you're running for your life from five armed men."

She blinked. "If you're saying my sister is trying to kill me, you're completely off base. She's a kid. And she didn't break in. She had a key."

"How old?"

"Excuse me?"

"How old is your *kid* sister?"

Harper hesitated, her face warming. "Twenty."

"Not a kid then."

She crossed her arms, winced when she pressed against her bruises, and dropped her arms to her sides.

The detective tapped the pen on his pad. "Sounds to me like there's someone else in your family who may have wanted to send those mercenaries after you. Except, I imagine if that's the case then the target would have been Bishop. Unless there's another reason your father might want you dead?"

She gasped. "My father? Now you're thinking he's the one who sent someone to kill me? Or Gage? That's—"

"Crazy," Gage supplied. "Completely out of character for the former president."

"Convince me."

"He loves me," Harper exclaimed. "He loves all his children. He would never do anything to hurt us."

Radley shrugged. "He's also a hard-nosed, unyielding narcissist, if the news reports from the past eight years are even a little bit accurate. And he's extremely tightfisted with his money even though he's a millionaire."

She clasped her hands together. It was either that or punch him. "He's far from perfect. But he's an excellent father. And if we truly need anything, he's more than happy to provide it. He just prefers that his children be independent and make their own way. I assure you, he wouldn't send gunmen after me."

"What about sending them after Bishop? You already admitted your father doesn't like him."

She shook her head. "He wouldn't. Not even against his worst enemy. He has a strong legacy of supporting law enforcement in his political career. He's an honorable man and wouldn't do something like that."

"Like I said. I need convincing. Bishop, you said it's out of character for him. Explain that."

"You already hit the nail on the head. He's a narcissist."

Harper sucked in a sharp breath.

Gage gave her an apologetic look. "You know it's true. Detective Radley, the most important thing in the world to Earl Manning is Earl Manning. Above all else, he wants to protect his reputation, his precious legacy as president. He'd never do anything to jeopardize that. I'll bet one of his own family members could be kidnapped and he wouldn't dare involve the FBI or anyone else to try to ransom them if there was any chance of it getting out into the media. It would destroy his reputation of being hard on crime and refusing to negotiate with criminals."

Harper's mouth fell open.

He quirked a brow, as if daring her to contradict him.

She couldn't believe he'd said those things. But if she tried to deny it, she'd be the hypocrite. He was, after all, right. Her father had done exactly what Gage had said. He'd offered money and Gage as his scapegoat to find his grandson. But he'd refused to involve anyone else for fear of harming his precious reputation.

The detective was writing notes in his little book and seemed to miss the nonverbal exchange between the two of them, which was probably a good thing. She didn't want to raise his suspicions any more than they already were about her family.

He stopped writing and eyed Gage. "I don't think you fleshed out that train of thought, but I think I followed it. You don't think the former president would hire thugs to kill either you or Harper for any reason because it could harm his reputation if things went bad. And that's more important to him than any grudge?"

"Absolutely."

"What about you, Ms. Manning? Do you agree with that assessment?"

She hesitated, still smarting over Gage's characterization of her father. But she couldn't ignore the truth, either. "Yes. I agree. My father isn't the one you're looking for."

"I think it's safe to assume your eleven-year-old half brother isn't part of this. That leaves your stepsister and stepmother as persons of interest."

Harper threw up her hands. "Enough. Okay? Leave my family out of this. They're good people." She glared at Gage, daring him to say otherwise. "My family's not perfect, my father least of all. But we love each other. We're very close. And, get real. It's not like we have mercenaries on speed dial. Who the heck hires five gunmen like that? I wouldn't know where to begin."

"It's easier than you think, Ms. Manning. Your father's anticrime platform means he's been heavily involved in investigations and cases against criminals. All he'd have to do is go through some old files he probably has in his home office right now and pull out names of some of the worst. He can afford any fee they'd charge. Wouldn't be hard to toss some money around to get the job done."

"I'm through talking with you about my family," she snapped.

"Fair enough." Radley didn't seem bothered by her anger and simply skimmed through his notes before continuing. "Moving on. We know Carter was alive around noon. As long as your sister corroborates that, and other people were with you from then on—which we'll need to establish, as well—you're in the clear for his murder."

"Well, thanks for that, I guess."

"But you're not, Bishop. Not until I get a timeline on you. Did you and the Seekers arrive together? Can they vouch for you?"

It was Gage's turn to cross his arms. "No. They can't. I took a shortcut, came up on the other side of the French Broad River in my car, parked at a campground and rented a canoe to take to Harper's place. I was already there when her sister arrived and I hid in a back room until she left. The Seekers arrived shortly after Cynthia and her boyfriend were gone. Since we established that Carter came over to see Harper while I was inside the house, obviously I'm not the killer."

The ambulance slowed then bumped and squeaked as it turned into the hospital drive that led to the emergency room entrance.

Radley's phone buzzed in his pocket. He read the message on the screen and tapped a reply before putting it away. He glanced from one to the other. "Why do I feel I'm being played here?"

Harper blinked and shot a glance at Bishop. But he didn't seem shaken at all.

"Just find the fifth gunman," Bishop told him. "Maybe you'll get lucky and he'll confess to killing Carter. Then he can tell you who hired him to kill Ms. Manning."

The ambulance parked and the cab's doors slammed shut as the EMTs got out. A few seconds later, the rear doors swung open to reveal the EMTs standing outside.

Detective Radley hopped out first. "Looks like I might get a chance to do exactly that—talk to the gunman. They captured him after a brief gunfight. They're bringing him here right now, to this hospital."

Chapter Seventeen

Harper blinked at the morning sun coming through the window blinds. The hospital was full so she'd been relegated to spend the entire night in the emergency ward, getting IV antibiotics and hoping the doctor would eventually agree to let her go home. Knowing she was the former president's daughter seemed to make everyone around her paranoid. They checked on her constantly and she suspected she was receiving far more care than she required.

Case in point, the day-shift nurse was hanging yet another IV bag on the pole beside her bed. How much fluid did one person need because they'd swallowed a thimbleful of brackish water?

The nurse set the call button on top of the blanket, next to Harper's hand, and smiled. "Need anything else? Perhaps another pillow?"

She had three already.

"No thank you. I'm good."

"Excellent. I'll check back in a bit."

"Take your time. Really."

The nurse's smile dimmed.

Harper immediately regretted her aggravated tone.

"Sorry. I'm a bit stressed out. I really do appreciate everything you're all doing for me."

The nurse's smile kicked up to full wattage. "It's my pleasure to help in any way I can. As I said, I'll check back in a little while. In the meantime, there's an extremely handsome man waiting in the hall to see you. If you're not up for company, I'd be happy to keep him occupied." She grinned and fanned herself.

Harper couldn't help laughing in spite of the past few days being some of the most trying days ever. "Is his name Gage Bishop?"

"If I say no, do I get to keep him?"

Her annoyance with the nurse returned, tenfold. It was a struggle to keep her smile intact. "Thanks for the offer. But you can send him in."

"You got it." She held the curtain back and stepped out of the room.

A moment later, a knock sounded on the wall that separated Harper's room from the next one.

"Come in," Harper called out.

The curtain billowed to the side and Gage stepped in, looking just as mouthwatering as ever. He adjusted the curtain closed behind him before heading to the bed. He winced when he saw the IV taped to the top of her right hand and the tube running up the pole.

"Still hooked up to that thing, I see. Weren't the antibiotics supposed to be finished early this morning?"

"They were. That's saline solution, or something like that. I'll bet you slept a lot better than I did. You go home after you disappeared?"

"I've been up all night working on your case. I went to Camelot to brainstorm with the other Seekers, aside from the ones rotating in and out to guard your room."

"And here I am, being completely ungrateful with everyone this morning. I'm sorry."

"No worries." He pulled up the only chair in the tiny room, an orange plastic one with chrome legs. Before sitting, he tested it first with his hands as if to ensure it would hold him. Then he carefully sat and rested his arms across the top of the bed rail. "What did the doctor say? How bad did I mess you up?"

"Mess me up?"

"Your ribs. The CPR."

She automatically placed her hand against the bruises on her chest, and noticed him wince again as if in empathy. She lowered her hand. "You didn't mess me up, Gage. You saved my life—something I should have thanked you for long ago. Thank you. I mean it. I can't count how many times and how many ways you saved my life. I'd be dead right now if it wasn't for you."

He took her left hand in both of his. "Don't talk like that."

She swallowed, content to enjoy the rush of awareness that shot through her at his unexpected touch. He pulled his hands back, as if suddenly realizing what he was doing, and rested his arms on the rail again. The loss of his warmth was like an ache in her heart.

"You didn't answer my question," he said. "Does that mean I *did* crack some ribs?"

"No, no. The X-rays came back clean. I'm totally okay. Lying in this bed seems silly, honestly. But they won't let me go until the doctor gives the all-clear. He's supposed to make his rounds in an hour or so." She glanced at the curtain then lowered her voice. "What about the gunman? Is he talking? Who hired him? Was it Sam or someone else? When will—?"

He smiled and put his hand on hers again. "I think you lost me about three questions back."

"Sorry, I just… I'm worried. About Shane. We've only got one more day left. The kidnapper is supposed to make contact tomorrow."

His smile faded. "That's why we've all been up working the investigation. Mason's got Seekers looking into this from every angle." He scrubbed his jaw, then leaned on the railing again. "Let's see, the lab results should be back soon. That's taking a little longer than I expected, considering the money Mason's throwing their way. No luck with the post office surveillance, as I'd feared. The printer metadata is taking longer than expected, too. We're still waiting on the company to get back to us with customer purchase records. Mason's got a judge leaning on them for the information."

"A judge? Wow."

"Never underestimate what Mason can get done outside of the legal system."

"What about the linguist?" she asked.

"Her report wasn't as helpful as I'd hoped. It doesn't rule anyone in or out on our potential suspect list."

Harper gave him an aggravated look. "Let me guess. The profile matches everyone in my family."

"Bingo."

She rolled her eyes.

"As for the gunman," Gage continued, "we're in luck there. He was shot, but it was a through-and-through, a flesh wound on his side. They stitched him up right in the emergency room. Didn't require surgery. But he's been sick ever since, throwing up, running a fever. They're pumping him with fluids and keeping him sedated to try to calm his system down. He's still here, in the ER, down the hall. As soon as he's better and in a room upstairs, the Seekers will interrogate him and figure out who hired him."

"Interrogate him? How? I can't see Detective Radley allowing that."

"Radley won't even know about it." He winked.

She couldn't help smiling. "I guess there are perks to being a Seeker. Other team members to create diversions, things like that. You said the gunman's down the hall?"

His expression turned serious again. "Don't worry. You're safe. Dalton and Eli were with the police when they brought him in. Eli's standing guard outside your door right now and he's not going anywhere. And a policeman is watching the gunman's room. He's also handcuffed to his bed. He's not going anywhere."

Harper nodded, but it was hard not to worry. One of the men who'd tried to kill her and Gage was in the same emergency ward as she was. It felt surreal. And scary.

A knock sounded. Gage stiffened, his hand going to his side. It dawned on her he was wearing a clean suit again, with a jacket, and whoever had brought him the clothes had likely also brought him a gun. What shenanigans had he pulled to be able to wear it in the hospital she wondered?

"Who is it?" he called out.

"Eli." He leaned inside the curtain, nodding at Harper. "Your family's here again to see you. Is it okay to let them in?"

A woman's voice called out from the other side of the curtain. "Well, of course it's okay to let us in."

The curtain billowed and Julia breezed in, followed by Cynthia and her boyfriend, Dean.

Gage let his jacket close over his holster and joined Eli by the doorway. He whispered something and Eli disappeared.

"You poor thing." Julia hurried to Harper's bedside and kissed the top of her head before gently taking her hand in hers, careful not to touch where the IV tubing was taped on top. "I can't believe how bold burglars have gotten these days. To break into your home with guns and go after you—"

"Oh please," Cynthia said from the other side of the bed. "I told you last night they weren't burglars. Dad said Bishop told him over the phone that they were mercenaries or something like that. Someone paid them to kill her, just like that guy that went after Dad."

Julia rested her head against Harper's pillow as she gave her a gentle hug. "Hired killers? What is this world coming to that a former president and his family are targets like this?"

Harper patted Julia's hand. "Please stop worrying. I'm okay. Gage saved my life and he's not going to let anything happen to me."

Cynthia grinned at Gage, who was leaning against the wall by the curtain silently watching them. Her gaze slid down to his shoes and she slyly glanced at Harper.

Don't you dare, Harper silently mouthed to her.

Her sister shrugged and pushed away from the wall. "Dean overheard some cops talking in the waiting room bathrooms before we left last night. They said some guy took out four gunmen all by himself. I'm guessing we all know who that was." She winked. "There was another one, though, right? He got away, but then the police caught him. Is he in the ER? Is that why there's a cop outside another curtained room a few down from this one?"

Julia's head shot up. "They caught one? And he's here?" She sounded horrified. "Bishop, what are you doing about that? He could come after Harper."

"I'm not in any danger," Harper assured her, trying to keep Gage from having to deal with her highly emotional stepmom. "Like Cynthia said, there's a policeman outside his room. Thanks to Gage, there's always a Seeker guarding my room, too. I'm perfectly safe. And I'll be leaving soon, once the doctor makes his rounds."

Julia looked up at the pole, frowning. "Why are you still getting an IV? I thought you were just having your ribs checked and you had to stay overnight for observation. Is something else wrong? Are you sick?" She pressed a hand against Harper's forehead.

Cynthia rolled her eyes. "The drama is only going to get worse once Dad gets here."

Harper's stomach jumped. "Please tell me you're kidding. He can't come here. This place will become a zoo with all those Secret Service agents milling around and stopping everyone."

"Welcome to my world," her sister said. "I'm living it every day. Can't wait for the fall semester to start up so I can escape back to campus."

Julia patted Harper's hand. "Cynthia's teasing you. Your father's still working with the FBI and Secret

Service on the investigation into the assassination attempt. He couldn't get away, but he sends his love."

Harper let out a pent-up breath, relieved.

"Surprise, surprise," Cynthia mocked. "The king couldn't tear himself away from his admirers to check on his daughter who was nearly killed."

"Cynthia," Julia warned.

"Relax, mommy dearest." She scooted around the end of the bed and motioned for Dean to come with her. "Let's check out the vending machines and see if there are any chocolate doughnuts. I love those things. We'll grab a soda, too. Harper, you want us to bring you something back?"

"No thanks. With everything that's happened, I don't think I could eat right now." She'd had some hospital food last night. But after realizing this morning that they only really had one more day until the kidnapper was supposed to contact them, she'd lost any appetite she'd woken up with.

Gage must have been worrying about Shane, as well, from the grim look on his face as he held back the curtain for Cynthia and her boyfriend.

Harper wanted to ask him questions about strategy, what they should do in regard to the kidnapper and steering the message the media would take on all of this. But she was stuck consoling Julia and giving her a much watered-down version of what had happened.

Eli came in with two more orange plastic chairs and set them against the wall. Harper smiled her thanks at him and Gage, knowing full well that must have been what Gage had whispered to Eli earlier. In spite of his sometimes gruff exterior and all the baggage between them, Gage was a gentleman at heart. Always had been.

A few minutes after Eli left the room to take up guard duty again, another knock sounded. Gage lifted the curtain back, revealing Dalton and Caleb, who both waved at Harper. She smiled in return, but couldn't wave. Julia was holding both her hands as she went on and on about how unsafe the world was.

The Seekers spoke in low tones to each other. At first, Gage shook his head no to whatever Dalton was telling him. But finally he nodded. The others stepped back and Gage let the curtain close. He strode to the other side of the bed and grasped the railing.

"Sorry to interrupt," he said, startling Julia, who apparently hadn't even realized he was standing across from her.

"Is something wrong?" she asked. "Oh my, has that bad man escaped?"

"No, ma'am. Harper, I've got both Eli and Caleb outside your room. Mason's here and needs to talk to me. He has some updates on—ah, a case we're working on. I need to step out for a few minutes."

Julia crossed her arms. "You're leaving? With that awful man just a few feet down the hall? Don't you care what happens to my daughter?"

Harper gasped. "Julia, don't—"

"It's okay," Gage said. "Ma'am, I assure you, I care *very much* about what happens to Harper. That's why there are two Seekers outside her room. And the gunman isn't a few feet away. He's around the corner, with a police guard."

Julia shook her head and looked away.

"Harper," Gage said. "Are you okay with this? If not, I'll tell Mason—"

"I'm more than okay with it," she assured him, still

feeling surprisingly touched by his saying he cared *very much* about what happened to her. "I know you're working an important case, right?"

He gave her a subtle nod, confirming what she'd thought. Whatever Mason was about to tell him had something to do with Shane.

Chapter Eighteen

Bishop jogged across the ER parking lot and rounded the end of the building. Dalton and Mason were waiting for him by a retention pond dotted with ducks and geese, near a stand of thick oak trees.

He shook Mason's hand. "Thanks for everything you're doing, that all the Seekers are doing to help."

"We're family," Mason said. "When one of us is hurting, we're all hurting."

Dalton nodded. "I almost lost Hayley last year. I know what you're going through with Harper and Shane. You can count on me, no matter what."

Bishop gripped his shoulder in a show of solidarity. "Harper and I aren't a couple. But I appreciate what you're saying." He chose to ignore their disbelieving looks. Until this case was settled, he needed to stay focused. It was going to be hard enough to do that today without having slept. Letting loose the floodgates of his feelings for Harper right now would emotionally wreck him. He had to keep it professional, for both their sakes, at least until they got Shane home safely. Then, well, all bets were off.

"I want to get back as soon as I can. Harper's stepmother's crying all over her and I don't trust her sister's boyfriend. He's way too quiet. I can't figure out if he's an introvert or busy scheming."

"We'll be quick," Mason assured him. "I assigned Bryson to try to locate the midwife. He couldn't find a Colette Proust anywhere around here, unsurprising since Earl Manning's lawyer couldn't, either. So, instead of starting with the present day and working backward, Bryson started with what was known about her six years ago. She lived in an apartment with her brother, Victor, until she moved in with Harper. A few weeks after she left Harper's place, she and Victor disappeared."

"Both of them?"

He nodded.

"Were they in on it together then? They moved to another town?"

"That was Bryson's assumption at first. But after conducting a thorough search of tax rolls in neighboring counties without any luck, he looked through surrounding states. Still nothing. He took a chance that someone in the apartment complex where the Prousts had lived might remember them. Sure enough, the property manager who was there during that time is still there, although just as a resident now. But she remembered them. Apparently, the brother was quite eccentric, which made them stand out in her mind. She said that at the end of their lease, which was right around the timeframe we're looking at, they planned on moving back home, to Paris."

"Paris?" Dalton and Bishop both said together.

"*The* Paris, as in France?" Bishop added.

"One and the same. Bryson couldn't get flight records going back that far, but he successfully located the brother, Victor, who is right now living in an apartment in the City of Lights."

"And Colette? Shane?" Bishop asked, hoping by some miracle Bryson had managed to find his son.

Mason shook his head. "Sorry. Bryson pulled some strings, used contacts he made while with the FBI, and had some constables do a wellness check on Victor. A very thorough one. They searched his entire home, top to bottom and even neighboring apartments. There are no signs of any children ever having lived with him. Interviews with his neighbors say he lives alone, rarely has any visitors. As for his sister, I'm afraid I don't have good news there, either. She became violently ill during the flight to France all those years ago. An ambulance was waiting for her when the plane landed. They rushed her to the hospital but couldn't save her. She had a massive heart attack."

Bishop swore. "Let me guess. Victor never heard of Shane or Harper."

"On the contrary. He knew his sister was staying with Harper. It was a lucrative arrangement and both of them were benefitting from it. But at the end of the pregnancy, Colette told him the same thing she told Harper, that Shane had died. The French authorities believed him, said there were no signs of subterfuge. Or, at least, no evidence that would justify them pursuing the matter any further."

Dalton crossed his arms. "Sounds like it's unlikely the Prousts were involved. So what are we looking at? Someone at the hospital stole Shane and said he'd died?"

"I don't buy it," Bishop said. "Colette just happens to bring a baby in distress to the emergency room and someone tells her he died? Then provides a death certificate, and yet she's not involved? You saw what it's like in the ER here. Tons of people all over the place going in and out of rooms. It would have to be a vast conspiracy. No, I think she was in on it but her brother didn't know.

"And even if I'm wrong, it makes sense to keep investigating that avenue to see where it leads. If she planned on using Shane to extort money, or even if she just wanted to raise him as her own, she'd have had to keep him with someone else for at least a little while so her brother wouldn't find out. Maybe she was going to come back for him later. But when she didn't return, why would whoever was watching Shane keep him for five years and then try to cash in on the opportunity? It doesn't make sense."

"Bryson pretty much said the same things you did when talking it through with me. And then he reminded me of what we all know but sometimes forget. When things start getting too complicated, they—"

"Probably aren't complicated at all," Bishop interjected, finishing his sentence. "We need to look at the simplest, most straightforward explanation."

"What would that be?" Dalton asked. "I'm not seeing anything simple about any of this."

Mason arched a brow and waited for Bishop.

"The simplest explanation is that Colette lied to Harper. The baby wasn't in distress. She used that as a ruse to take the baby wherever she'd planned to take him."

Dalton scratched his chin. "That eliminates the idea of a hospital conspiracy, which definitely simplifies things. But we still have a death certificate to explain. Where did that come from? You think Colette forged it?"

"Most likely," Mason said. "She probably had it ready the whole time. All she had to do was to fill in the date once the baby was born. And since Harper's father had gone to such lengths to hire Colette and keep everything a secret, there'd be no reason for Harper to doubt Colette or the validity of the document."

Bishop dragged a hand through his already disheveled hair. "If that's the case, then Colette planned this from day one, and never intended to take Shane with her to Paris. So what was her angle? An illegal private adoption to make a few bucks on the side? Then years later, whoever adopted him somehow figured out who his biological mother is and decided to cash in on it?"

Dalton shook his head. "That's really messed up. Who'd keep a kid for five years then offer him up for money?"

"Maybe they don't plan to make the exchange," Bishop said. "Maybe they're hoping to keep Shane and disappear with the money."

"That's certainly a possibility," Mason concurred. "Bryson's working the money angle, looking for an electronic trail, interviewing anyone who used to know the Prousts, so he can see if one of her associates mysteriously disappeared around the time Colette left, perhaps with a newborn baby. If someone paid her, he'll find the transaction and figure out who's behind it."

Bishop fisted his hands at his sides. "We still don't have an explanation for the mercenaries. Who hired them? Why kill Harper before getting the ransom for Shane? Once again, it doesn't make sense."

Dalton shifted on his feet. "If the puzzle piece

doesn't fit, maybe it's the wrong puzzle. I know we all agree it seems unlikely, but the gunman aspect may really have nothing to do with Shane and the ransom. Maybe for the time being we assume it's related to the assassination attempt on former president Manning and focus on the kidnapping, especially since the exchange is supposed to take place tomorrow."

"That's actually a good idea," Mason said. "Shane should be the primary focus right now."

"I wish we could keep all of this about the gunmen quiet," Bishop added. "But there are too many bodies, too many cops involved, to keep this fiasco out of the press. If, by some miracle, it's not related to the ransom scheme, I sure hope this Sam guy doesn't get too nervous and call the whole thing off."

Mason shook his head. "I don't think he will." He exchanged a quick glance with Dalton.

Bishop narrowed his eyes. "What? There's something else, isn't there? Another reason you wanted to meet with me?"

Mason gave him a curt nod. "There is one more thing. The lab I hired is still rerunning the actual DNA tests. But they already did a quick paper-only review of the work the other lab did, a scientific walk-through of their methods, their analysis and conclusions. They reviewed the DNA profiles in the report and agreed that, based on those profiles, and the other tests that were done, the samples are mother and son, and the son's sample came from a live person."

When Mason didn't say anything else, Bishop pressed forward. "That confirms what we already believed to be true. Why do you look all gloom and doom? What's going on?"

Mason huffed out a long breath. "I want any testing the lab does for us to be as thorough and accurate as possible. They're retesting the sample of Shane's hair, as you asked. In the meantime, since a mother-son relationship was proved by the earlier testing, I felt it only made sense to make an additional comparison—to the alleged father."

Bishop stared at him incredulously. "You ran a paternity test? What'd you do, use my DNA profile on file with the Seekers, without my permission?"

"I did what I felt was necessary to protect my employee, and friend, from potentially being taken advantage of."

Bishop's stomach sank as he waited for the rest. "Just say it."

"I had the results double-checked, just to be certain. There is no mistake. Based on your DNA profile, there's no way that you can be Shane's father."

It felt like the air was being sucked from his lungs. He shook his head, his heart refusing to accept what Mason was telling him. But it made sense if he looked at the simplest explanation. He couldn't remember making love to Harper in the pool house because it never happened. She'd gotten pregnant with another man's child, just as he'd believed for years, until she'd convinced him otherwise in Gatlinburg. But why would she do that, drag him back into her life years later? Convince him he was her child's father? Was it just to ensure that he would help her get Shane back? So she could keep everything out of the media but have someone with the background, and incentive, to save Shane without telling anyone what had happened?

"No. I saw the picture. I texted you a copy. Shane

has the same birthmark on his face that all of the men in my family have."

"Pictures can be faked," Mason said. "You know that."

He shook his head again. "You didn't see her in that conference room, the fear and grief in her eyes, in her voice. If she was lying, then she deserves an award. Because I bought every single line."

Dalton frowned. "I don't know, Mason. Harper didn't strike me as the kind of person who would do that."

Bishop closed his eyes, letting what he knew, what he didn't know, and what he suspected, flow through his mind. The clues bumped against each other until they all coalesced into one picture. He'd been such a fool. He opened his eyes. "It makes sense," he said quietly. "It simplifies everything."

"How so?" Dalton asked.

"Look at the simplest explanation for all of this," Bishop said. "There was no conspiracy between Colette and someone else. No fake adoption. Shane really was in distress. Colette really took him to the hospital where he…where he died. The ransom note is fake. There is no Sam. There's only Harper."

Dalton looked at him in disbelief. "No way. That can't be right. She's already wealthy. She wouldn't need to pull something like this to get money."

"She's not rich," Mason said, his voice subdued. "Her father is. And he's tight with the purse strings. He insists that his children make their own way in the world, like he did. But most of former president Manning's assets aren't liquid. We've been running financials on him as part of the investigation. He's struggling to raise the money to pay the ransom. Harper's very close to him. She'd likely know it would be difficult for him to come up with the money."

"That's why she involved me," Bishop said. "In theory, anyway. It also means she's kept tabs on me for years, found out I own a lucrative construction company on top of being a Seeker. She figured I'd be able to come up with the money. I already told her I'm paying the ransom."

Dalton held up his hands. "Hold it. Before you go off that deep end, there's one very big glaring hole in your theory. The lab said the hair samples are mother and son. And that the sample came from a living child. How do you explain that if Shane died at birth?"

Mason looked at Bishop. "If we assume the theory you just put forth is fact, then, again, the simplest explanation is that the child's hair samples weren't from Shane. And the mother's weren't from Harper. They're from some other mother and son."

"Which means your theory that I'm not the father could be wrong, as well. Apples and oranges."

Mason nodded reluctantly. "Agreed. We don't have Harper's DNA profile to compare. But it wouldn't be difficult to get a blood sample while she's in the hospital. She wouldn't know it was for a DNA test. I can make it happen. If you're okay with it."

Bishop stared at the pond for a long moment before giving him a curt nod. "Go ahead. But tell Bryson to keep digging. Tell *all* the Seekers to keep digging. I have to know for sure what's really going on and I'm too tired right now to know what to believe." He met Dalton's gaze. "I agree with you about Harper. She's a good person. It's hard to believe she'd try to pull a stunt like this. That she'd purposely hurt me, or anyone else. Until or unless I have incontrovertible proof to the contrary, I choose to believe that she's not trying to rip my heart out, that Shane is still alive, and that he's my son."

He turned to leave then froze. A man had just stepped out from behind one of the oak trees.

Detective Radley.

"Hello, gentlemen. Nice weather out here, isn't it?" He motioned to the pond. "And a gorgeous place to take a break from all the craziness going on inside."

A feeling of dread settled in Bishop's gut as he exchanged a quick glance with Mason and Dalton.

"Don't worry. There's no one else out here, just me, standing behind the trees when you three came out to have your little huddle. I was going to announce my presence but once you started talking, I was too stunned to stop you." Radley smiled. "Let me see if I have this right. Harper was single and pregnant and tried to hide it. I assume to keep from embarrassing a sitting president. A little old-fashioned if you ask me, but whatever. She was secluded somewhere with a midwife, this Colette Proust you spoke about. Then she thought the baby, Shane, died. But years later, someone is trying to say Shane is alive and wants to trade him for ransom. Or, in your alternate theory, the baby did die and Harper's just some money-grubbing treasure hunter out for a quick buck."

Bishop winced.

"Oh, wait," Radley added. "I forgot the part where Shane may or may not be your son. Does that pretty much sum it up?"

Bishop took a menacing step forward, but Dalton stepped between them.

Radley held up his hands in a placating gesture. "In spite of what it probably looks like to you, I'm not your enemy. I'm not the media or some paparazzi trying to sell a story. I'm just here to solve a murder. Blake Carter's murder. And of course, I need some kind of explanation for why I have four dead gunmen in the morgue and another guy in the ER.

"If you cooperate with me," he asserted, "you'd be surprised what kind of damage control and manipulation of the press that I can do. But I can't help you if you don't help me. I need information. If you're dealing with extortion and kidnapping, that's exactly the kind of thing that might explain a bunch of mercenaries being involved, and it could explain Mr. Carter's murder if he saw something he shouldn't have. Or maybe he was part of the kidnapping plot. Did that theory occur to any of you?"

None of them said anything.

"Okay. How about this?" Radley tried again. "How much money are we talking about here? Would it be enough incentive for daddy dearest to hire gunmen to kill his daughter so he wouldn't have to pay? Or maybe he was more concerned with protecting his crime-fighting legacy in the court of public opinion than trying to ransom a grandson he never acknowledged he had. Please tell me one of you Seekers has thought of those possibilities." He glanced at each of them. "Anyone? Bueller?" He chuckled at his reference to the movie from the eighties. The rest of them weren't laughing.

"There's another theory that comes to mind," he

continued, as if they were all best friends chatting on a golf course about which club to use for the next hole. "What if the hair samples are indeed fake, as you've theorized, but Harper doesn't know that? What if, instead of her playing you, someone else is playing her?"

Bishop was about to tell Radley where he could go with all his theories when his phone buzzed in his pocket.

All of their phones were buzzing.

They pulled them out and read the messages on their screens. Then, as one, they took off running for the emergency room.

Chapter Nineteen

The curtains billowed in the doorway of Harper's room as more people ran down the hallway outside it. Eli stood by the curtain, his back to the wall, pistol in his right hand pointing down at the floor as he peered out the crack. Caleb had shoved Harper's bed against the wall on the left, as far from the curtained doorway as he could get it. And he, too, stood guard, at the foot of her bed, gun in hand as he kept himself between her and the doorway.

Her frustration mounted as she clutched the bed rail, keeping quiet as they'd ordered her the moment code blue was called on Room 14. Was that the gunman's room? Even if it was, why were Caleb and Eli acting as if they thought a battalion was about to lay siege to her room?

The curtain billowed again. She leaned to the side to look around Caleb and saw Gage standing just inside the room. He cast a quick glance her way then spoke in low tones to Eli. Before she could ask him what was going on, he slipped back out and Eli jerked the curtain almost all the way shut again, leaving only a slit for him to keep an eye on what was happening outside her room.

Just when Harper was ready to hop off the bed and try to make a jail break, Gage entered the room again. This time, when he spoke to Eli, Eli holstered his gun and stepped outside the curtain. Gage strode to the bed and sent Caleb out, as well. He eyed the wonky way the bed was pressed up against the wall and gave her what seemed to be a reluctant smile.

"Want me to straighten out your bed?"

"I want you to tell me what's going on."

He rolled the bed back into position and slid the three orange guest chairs all on the far side of the bed, closest to the door, before taking up a stance on the other side, his back to the wall. "Our gunman had a medical emergency. Caleb and Eli guarded you in case it was a diversion so someone could slip inside your room."

She stared at him in surprise. "Was it? A diversion?"

"Not as far as I can tell. No one tried to get past Eli."

"And?"

"And what?"

She sighed. "You're being awfully tight-lipped. What happened? Is the gunman okay?"

"They couldn't revive him."

She pressed her hand against her chest. "What happened? Were his injuries worse than the doctors realized?"

"No one's sure at this point. But it looks like a heart attack."

"Looks like?"

Before he could respond, a knock sounded. Eli moved the curtain to let her stepmother and Secret Service agent Faulk into the room. Her mother was smiling and holding two cups of coffee, but stopped when she saw them, her smile fading.

"Is something wrong?" she asked. "You both look like someone kicked your favorite dog."

Harper started to reassure her but Gage spoke first.

"Faulk, I heard you were assigned to protect Mrs. Manning these days. Where were you earlier this morning when she was here alone?"

The agent stopped, his eyes widening. "I was told she was being looked after by your team, so I went to the cafeteria. Was there a problem?"

"Leave him alone, Bishop." Julia headed to the bed and set the coffee cups on the tray beside it. "You're not a Secret Service agent anymore, so it's none of your concern."

"Julia," Harper chastised, "don't speak that way to Gage."

"It's okay," Gage assured her. "Where have you been, Mrs. Manning? You missed the excitement."

She frowned and gestured at the coffee cups. "I think it's obvious where I've been. I wanted to get my daughter a decent cup of coffee. That stuff at the nurse's station is awful. The cafeteria's not much better. I threw some cream and sugar in to hopefully make it drinkable. Why? What did I miss?"

Another knock sounded and this time Cynthia and Dean entered the room, each of them carrying a soda and a small bag, presumably of snacks. Cynthia had been smiling at her boyfriend but her smile disappeared when she stopped at the end of the bed, looking at each of them. "Who died?"

"Interesting you should ask," Gage said. "The gunman just passed away. I'll ask you and Dean the same question I just asked your mother. Where did you two disappear to for so long? You both left before me and I've been gone far longer than I expected. The vending machines aren't that far away."

Cynthia rolled her eyes, unfazed, and crossed to the other side of the bed. "I think your boyfriend is accusing us of having something to do with that slimeball's death."

Julia gasped. "Bishop, how dare you—"

"Julia," Harper interrupted. "Cynthia, everyone, would you please give me and Gage a few moments alone?"

Her stepmother sputtered in outrage. Cynthia grabbed her arm and hauled her toward the doorway, with Faulk and Dean following behind.

"Come on, Mom. Harper's had enough of your drama for one morning." She winked at Harper, earning a glare from her mom.

When they were gone, and the sound of their bickering faded down the hall, Harper threw the covers off and wrestled the railing down so she could sit on the side of the bed. "My sister got that part right, for sure. I'm tired of drama. Of all the drama. Tired of being told to be quiet and treated like a child who can't handle the truth. And I don't appreciate you practically accusing my family of murder. Even if they were cold, bloodthirsty killers, how would they have gotten into the gunman's room, much less caused him to have a heart attack?"

"He was sedated and handcuffed to the bed. Apparently, that was enough for the cop guarding his room to leave his post and flirt with the nurses at the nursing station farther down the hall. Anyone could have slipped inside his room."

"Check the cameras," she snapped. "Those little surveillance bubbles on the ceiling are all over this place. Then once you see my mom and sister haven't gone near that man's room, you can come back and apologize. To all of us."

His jaw tightened. "Actually, checking the cameras was the first thing we did. But they're pointed at the main entrance to the ER corridor, not the entrances to each room."

"Okay. Then I'm sure you can clearly see when my mom and sister left and when they came back. Which was obviously after the code blue."

"Funny thing about that, too. There's a good ten-minute gap I can't account for in their movements around the hospital."

She blinked. "Good grief. You're serious, aren't you? You really think they could be involved."

He sighed and straightened. "As I've said before, everyone's a suspect. Anything is possible."

"Well, how about this as an explanation for that ten-minute gap. Knowing my mother and sister, they probably stopped at the waiting room inside the ER to argue about something stupid, as usual, before coming into my room."

"I'll be sure to ask them about it."

"Good grief."

The curtain slid back a few feet and a tech stepped into the room carrying vials of blood in a plastic tray. Behind him, Eli pulled the curtain closed again.

"Hello there." He smiled at both of them and set his tray on the end of the bed. "I'm here to take a

blood sample. Need to check your ID bracelet first."
He scanned the bar code on her wrist. "Let's see who
we have. Harper Manning?"

She nodded and confirmed her birth date. As the
tech drew the sample, she asked, "Why are you drawing blood when I'm supposed to get out of here soon?
Where's the doctor anyway? He should have been here
by now."

He shrugged. "I just follow the orders the doctors
write up. Sorry, ma'am. Maybe the nurses can answer
your questions."

"Thanks. I'll be sure to ask them."

Gage stood on the other side of the bed, watching
in silence.

The tech printed a label from the scanner and attached it to the blood vial, then gathered up his trash
and put it in the medical waste container attached to
the wall. "Thank you, Ms. Manning. I hope you feel
better soon."

She smiled her thanks. When he left, she pinned
Gage with a glare, ready to tear into him. But he was
already pushing away from the wall and heading for
the doorway.

"Gage, wait. We need to talk."

"I need to take care of a few things first." He
whipped the curtain back and left.

"Oh no you don't," she muttered. She slid to the edge
of the bed and yanked the tape off her IV.

Eli took a step forward as if to stop her. She narrowed her eyes in warning. He immediately retreated
to the curtain.

Biting her lip, she slowly pulled the plastic needle
out, then laid it with the tubing over the IV pump. After

locating her clothes in the closet, she tossed them on the bed and aimed a taunting look at Eli. He promptly stepped outside the room. Once dressed, she headed off into battle.

The battle lasted all of five seconds, the time it took for Eli to grab her arm in the hallway and pull her back into the room.

"Ms. Manning, I'm sorry. But I'm under strict orders to keep an eye on you."

She shoved his hand off her arm. "Keep an eye on me? Do you mean make sure I don't go into another patient's room and kill them?"

His eyes widened. "Um, no, ma'am. My orders are to protect you, to keep you safe."

"It's Eli, right?"

"Yes, ma'am."

She gritted her teeth. "Eli, I'm pretty sure you're older than me. Can we drop the ma'am?"

"Yes, ah, Ms. Manning."

She crossed her arms. "Where's Gage?"

"In a meeting."

"Another meeting? I'm sure it has to do with me. I'd like to join that meeting. Where is it?"

"I can't tell you that. But I assure you that he'll be back soon and—"

"Eli?"

"Yes?"

"If you don't take me to Gage right now, I'm going to open every door in this hospital until I find him. And if you grab my arm again or try to stop me in any way, my father's lawyers will slam you with an assault charge that will have you tied up in court for the next decade and drain all your assets. Pick a side, but do it fast. Because I'm leaving, Right now."

Chapter Twenty

After Eli led Harper down several hallways in the hospital, she was beginning to think he was calling her bluff about getting lawyers involved. In spite of her threat, she certainly had no intention to create legal problems for him. He and the other Seekers were risking their lives to help her. But it had been the only threat she could think of to get her back in the game instead of sitting—or in this case, lying—on the sidelines.

Just as she was ready to tell him he'd won this charade and to take her back to her room, he stopped. The door in front of them boasted a bright orange-and-white nameplate. The VOLS Conference Room was obviously a nod to Knoxville's University of Tennessee.

"I'll go in first," he said, "and give everyone a heads-up that you're here."

"No need. Thanks." She swept past him, entered the room, and stopped in surprise. The usual suspects were there. Mason, Caleb, Dalton and, of course, Gage, who was frowning at her from his seat directly across from the door. What she hadn't expected was the man sitting at the far right end of the long table—Detective Radley.

Gage stared at Eli. "Do you need my assistance in escorting Ms. Manning back to her room?"

Eli's face reddened. But before he could say anything, Harper pulled out the nearest chair and sat. "I'm not going anywhere. You don't get to practically accuse my stepmother and sister of murdering that gunman and then leave me out of a meeting about it. I want to know what's going on."

"Excellent," Detective Radley chimed in, much to Gage's obvious displeasure. "We were just discussing our John Doe gunman and the fact that we have a name for him now—Jerry Wallace. His fingerprints returned a match in the FBI's AFIS system. Wallace is an ex-con whose brother is still in prison, in large part because of strict mandatory sentencing laws championed by none other than your father, Earl Manning."

Harper stared at him in shock. "Then the men who tried to kill Gage and me...it was revenge, because of my father's policies? Wait, that means the attack at my house is related to the assassination attempt in Gatlinburg?"

Gage crossed his arms on top of the table. "We don't know yet. The Secret Service is looking into a possible connection and they're still investigating the man who tried to kill your father. Detective Radley is just throwing out potential links." He shot Radley a decidedly cool look. "Even though we've said repeatedly that we need to focus on other things right now, because of the tight deadline."

"The Secret Service is looking into the gunmen now? Good grief. This is much bigger than I'd realized." She swallowed hard. "Or hoped."

Gage tapped the table. "There are no secrets in this room, Harper. Radley knows about Shane."

She shot the detective another shocked glance. When he nodded, she tightened her fists beneath the table. "I don't understand. Why would you tell him that? You're jeopardizing our child's life."

"He didn't tell him." Mason, sitting to Gage's left, gave her an apologetic look. "I'm afraid in my eagerness to bring Bishop up to speed on some findings regarding your case, I didn't realize the detective was nearby—within hearing distance. He heard enough to guess the rest, so we're working together from here on out.

"Radley understands the need for discretion, that it's potentially a matter of life or death for…your son. The hope is that he can spin the information provided to the media to ensure that nothing about Shane and the ransom demand is revealed. For now, at least until we know all the facts of what's going on and who's behind it, the attack on you will be reported as part of a plot against the entire Manning family."

"Ms. Manning?"

She looked down the table at Radley.

"I promise you that I'll do everything in my power to keep the plot against your son quiet. No one wants to do anything that could jeopardize his life. On the other hand, as Bishop has emphatically pointed out, knowledge is power. You have a much better chance of a desirable outcome if we can figure out who the kidnapper is and rescue Shane before the appointed exchange. And that's exactly what we hope to do. We were just discussing what we know about the gunman since we still don't know for sure whether it's related to the ransom demand or not."

She rubbed her hands up and down her arms. "If you're trying to reassure me, you're doing a lousy job."

"We're trying to get to the facts," Gage said.

His demeanor was less hostile than when she'd first come into the room. But now it bordered on chilly. What had happened to the man who'd been so overcome with emotion over the knowledge that he had a son that his voice had sounded close to breaking? What had happened to the man who'd done everything he could to reassure her, and promised to keep her and Shane safe? She wanted that version of Gage back, wanted him to hold her, to make her feel safe again, and to fill her with hope. Something must have happened that had him angry with her. What was it?

Mason tapped the table this time, drawing everyone's attention. "Let's get back to the discussion at hand. Radley was filling us in about Wallace."

"There's not much more to tell," Radley said, "other than that he's a career criminal with an ax to grind against former president Manning. What's important is that the last physical he had during his most recent stint in jail showed he was quite healthy with no history, and no family history, of any kind of heart trouble. That is why I've instructed the medical examiner to cast a wide net of toxin testing on his blood. If someone gave him something to cause his heart attack, we want to know what it was." He paused briefly before adding, "I've also put the medical waste disposal container from his room into evidence. The state lab is backed up too much to help us with the tight window we have. So Mason's contacts at a private lab will process the evidence, examine any syringes inside the container and test those for toxins, too. If any are found, they'll swab for DNA to see if someone without gloves touched the syringe. No guarantees, but it's a solid place to start."

Harper looked at Gage. "Then you really do think someone poisoned him, gave him something to cause his heart attack?"

He shrugged. "It's the first thing that occurred to me, given his athletic build and the fact that he seemed in good health other than a fairly insignificant gunshot wound. It also seems suspicious that he's not the first person associated with you to have died of a heart attack. Colette Proust had a heart attack and passed away a few weeks after Shane's alleged death."

"Colette's dead?"

He nodded.

She stared at him a long moment, ruthlessly pushing back the shock and grief over Colette's death. She'd deal with those feelings later. "And you think— what?—that I'm somehow involved in her death, and this Wallace guy's death years later, because I'm *associated* with them?"

He frowned then shook his head. "I wasn't saying that. No one suspects you of being involved in their deaths."

Mason, Caleb, Dalton, even Eli, who'd taken a chair at the far left end of the table well away from her, all shook their heads, agreeing with Gage.

Radley, however, remained silent.

When she speared him with a questioning look, he held his hands up. "I'm just following the facts. I don't have any suspects yet. But I'm also not willing to rule anyone out."

She shoved her hair back from her face. "Can someone please tell me more about what happened to Colette?"

Gage brought her up to speed. "We don't have records from a doctor to state that she was healthy or what kind of cardiac history she might have had. But her brother doesn't recall any heart problems in the family. So Radley pulled some strings. And Bryson—another Justice Seeker with some international contacts—called in some favors and put some pressure on Victor, Colette's brother."

"Victor was more than willing to allow an exhumation after I wired an obscene amount of money to his account," Mason said. "It was much faster than obtaining a court order."

She gave him a weak smile. "Thank you. I don't know that I'll ever have an obscene amount of money to be able to repay you, though."

"It's not a loan, Ms. Manning. I don't expect repayment."

She knew it was because of his friend and employee, Gage. But she still appreciated that he'd gone all-in to help save Shane. "Thank you."

He nodded.

Gage took over the narrative again. "Colette's body will be tested for signs of poisoning, with particular emphasis on things that can mimic or cause a heart attack. If we find that poison played a role in her death, and Wallace's, and the same kind of poison was used, it will be hard to argue that their deaths are unrelated. As it is, given our severe time constraint with the ransom date looming, we're moving forward with the assumption that they were both killed by the same person.

We're looking into who could have interacted with both of them. And before you ask, yes, we're looking hard at your immediate family."

Harper started to argue, but he held up a hand to stop her.

"We're also looking at everyone who had access to your family during the time that you were pregnant. If your family isn't responsible for what happened to Colette, then someone close to them likely is—someone who overheard one of them talking about your situation."

She considered how cold he'd been to Faulk in her room earlier. "The Secret Service. You suspect them?"

"Faulk and Thompson are both high on my list of people we're looking into, especially Faulk since he was around during your pregnancy and recently popped back into your family's lives after being reassigned. The reason for his reassignment seems fuzzy at best, as if it's a cover to get him back at the Manning estate. I'm trying to get more information on that."

She sat in silence, letting it all sink in. The idea that people who'd sworn their own lives to keep her and her family safe could be the same people trying to kill her was sobering, to say the least.

A knock sounded on the door.

Caleb, to Harper's left, opened the door a crack then swung it wide to let the person in.

A tech in a white lab coat and green scrubs stepped inside carrying a familiar-looking tray with vials of blood and supplies. "I'm looking for Mr. Bishop?"

Gage held up his hand.

Harper watched in confusion as the tech rounded the table and prepped Gage for a blood draw. She glanced around the table, but no one would even look at her. Except Gage. He kept his gaze locked on hers the whole time the tech worked on him.

As soon as the tech left, Harper asked, "Why did he take your blood? My blood was drawn before I came here, even though I'm supposed to be discharged soon. I can't help but wonder if that's not a coincidence. What's going on?"

Mason stood and motioned to the other Seekers, who immediately exited the room. "Detective? If you have more questions, I'll address them. And Bishop has some suggestions he told me about before you joined us. I'll run those by you. Let's step outside."

Radley readily agreed and soon Harper was once again sitting alone in a conference room across from Gage. But this time, she wasn't there to plead her case or to ask for his help. This time he held all the cards. And she didn't even know what game they were playing.

"Gage?"

He started to say something, but seemed to think better of it. Instead, he rose, rounded the table and sat in the chair beside hers, swiveling it to face her.

"I don't know an easy way to tell you this, so I'll just say it. The Justice Seekers keep records of each employees' DNA profile, in case the worst happens and they need to identify…well, remains. Mason had a private lab compare my profile to the one from the lab your father hired. According to Mason's lab, Shane can't be my son."

She waited for him to say something more. Like, that he knew there'd been a mistake so he'd asked the lab to double-check the results. Or that he'd been with her nearly 24/7 for over two years and had reconciled his knowledge of her character with what she'd told him in Gatlinburg, and he realized how wrong he'd been all these years. She waited for him to assure her that it didn't matter what the lab said. Shane was his son. Their son. Forget the faulty lab. But he said nothing, and once again her heart fractured along one of those poorly healed cracks.

"You think I lied about that night in the pool house?"

He hesitated.

She pushed out of her chair and threw open the door.

He grabbed her arm, stopping her.

"Let me go." She desperately struggled to keep the threatening tears from falling.

"I will, but be warned. You're not leaving here without me by your side. Five armed men tried to kill you, and nearly did. Whatever threat you used on Eli won't work with me."

Her face heated. "I'm leaving. Tag along if you want, but don't expect me to talk to you. We're done."

He sighed heavily yet didn't let go of her arm. "You can't go home. It's a crime scene, and it's not safe there anyway."

"Then I'll go to a hotel."

He shook his head. "You'd be far too vulnerable. I have somewhere else in mind. The Manning family estate."

Her mouth dropped open and she looked up at him in spite of the tears she knew were shining in her eyes.

He frowned. "Harper? I should have been more diplomatic in how I said all that. I didn't mean to—"

"It doesn't matter. What matters is what you said about taking me to my father's home. It doesn't make sense. After saying you suspect my family, and the Secret Service agents assigned to guard them, you're going to take me right into the middle of all that?" To her horror, a tear slid down her cheek.

He winced and reached out as if to wipe it away.

She ducked back from his hand.

He grasped her shoulders. "We're running out of time to figure out who has Shane before we're completely at the kidnapper's mercy. I can't think of a better way to flush out whoever is behind this than to offer you as bait."

Her heart cracked even more at his declaration. "Why am I not surprised? Of course you'd offer me as bait. Now *that* goes along with the opinion you've always held of me. Because I don't matter."

"The hell you don't." He slammed the door shut and swung her around so that her back was against the conference room wall. She only had a second to register what was happening before he swooped down and captured her mouth with his.

She wanted to bite him, to hit him, to yell at him. No, she wanted to *want* to do those things. Instead, what she really wanted to do was to pull him close and drink him in. Her traitorous body did exactly that, melting against him and returning his fevered kiss with all the heat and passion banked inside her for the last six years.

Ever since that one night they'd shared in the pool house, she'd lived with the memory of how incredible they'd been together. Of how perfectly their bodies fit, like two pieces of the same puzzle, two halves of the same soul. And she'd craved recapturing that elusive magic again. She'd grieved his loss in her life and had longed for him after he'd left. But her memories had faded. They'd become a pale copy of what could be. Until now. All the emotions and lust and longing inside her was reawakened, and she couldn't get enough of him.

He groaned low in his throat, his tongue tangling with hers, his hands spearing through her hair as he moved his lips to her neck. When he lightly sucked, she had to bite down on her lip to keep from crying out at the sheer ecstasy of his touch. His hands slid down her back, caressing, stroking, learning her body all over again.

Then he swept her up in an even hotter kiss, making her practically weep with wanting him. He shuddered against her and pressed the entire length of his body into hers, pushing her hard against the wall.

A sharp pain shot through her ribs. She arched away from him, turning her head to the side.

He immediately stepped back, a look of chagrin on his face. "Did I hurt you? I'm so sorry. I forgot. Your ribs—"

"Are fine." She took a shallow breath and then another, riding through the pain.

He grabbed a chair, scooted it beside her and carefully helped her sit. He crouched in front of her, his face lined with concern. "Do you want me to call for a doctor?"

"No, no. Just…" She drew another shallow breath. "Just give me a moment. Apparently, the drugs they gave me are wearing off. Super bummer. Really *really* bad timing." She laughed and immediately grimaced at the protest her ribs made.

His hand shook as he gently feathered her hair back

from her face. "I'd never intentionally hurt you, Harper. I hope you believe that."

"I'm fine. Really. The pain's almost gone."

He took her hands in his. "It's not just the ribs I'm talking about. Mason is running fresh lab tests to validate the original ones. That's why the tech drew blood. Mason insisted and I'm way too tired to think straight. I was a fool to agree to it. But it doesn't matter. I don't care what those lab results say. Shane matters to me because he's yours. Whether I'm his father or not, I'm going to do everything in my power to rescue him and to keep you safe. I won't let any harm come to you."

She blinked, shock and hurt warring against each other as the euphoria of everything they'd just shared began to evaporate. He still didn't believe her. He thought she was lying, that Shane wasn't his. And he thought by saying he'd accept Shane as his own, even though he didn't believe he was, that it made everything okay between them.

He searched her gaze. "Are you sure you don't want me to get a doctor? You still seem to be in pain."

A doctor couldn't do anything for the type of pain she was feeling right now. She forced a smile and steeled herself against the urge to break down and weep for that tiny glimpse of a future between the two of them she'd foolishly pictured while in his arms.

"I'm okay. I'll just…head to my room and demand some discharge papers so I can get out of here."

He helped her stand. But before opening the door, he said, "I care about you, Harper. God help me, I always have. And I wouldn't do anything to put you in danger. Taking you to the Manning estate makes sense.

I'll explain why on our way. But I need you to trust me. Can you do that?"

Not with her heart. Never again. He'd proved he couldn't be trusted with that. She nodded, letting him make of it what he would.

He pulled open the door.

Chapter Twenty-One

As Gage performed a security check on all of the rooms throughout the Nashville Manning family home, Harper waited in the two-story foyer in front of the massive staircase, surrounded by gold-framed ancestral paintings dating back to the Revolutionary War. It was surreal being here again, even if for only a few days. The last time she was here, she'd wavered between the euphoric high of discovering that Shane might still be alive to a bottomless well of despair fearing that the whole thing was a hoax.

It was no hoax. The first lab had proved that. Or at least, she'd thought it had. But Mason's lab claimed that Gage wasn't Shane's father. She'd immediately assumed his lab was mistaken. After all, she knew for a fact that Gage was the father. But it was hard to believe that with the full resources of the Justice Seekers behind the lab, and so much riding on the results of the tests, that they'd be careless enough to make that kind of mistake. Other possibilities had crept insidiously through her mind, sinking the talons of doubt deep into her soul.

What if Mason's lab *hadn't* made a mistake?

The only way for that to be possible was if the hair sample from the ransom note wasn't Shane's.

She closed her eyes for a moment, trying to reason it all out. The first lab had done two tests, one on the hair sample from the note, and one from her. The conclusion was a mother-son relationship. That was what had proved to her that her son was still alive. That's what had given her hope. But Shane was the only child she'd had. If the hair wasn't from Shane, then the lab had to have made a mistake when testing *her* hair. Was it even possible for a lab to find a mother-son link between two DNA profiles if they weren't related? Was it possible for another lab *not* to find a father-son link between two DNA profiles if they *were* related?

It was all so confusing. She couldn't reconcile any of it, no matter how she looked at it. And nothing explained what had happened at her home, the attack by five gunmen who'd clearly been trying to kill her. Was that completely unrelated to the ransom demand? Or was it something far worse, something so sinister that goose bumps rose on her arms as she tested and weighed suspicions seeded by Gage's comments at the hospital?

Could someone in her own family want her dead?

As if against her will, her gaze was drawn to the right of the massive staircase to the open double door that led into her father's office. Not long ago, she'd gone into that cavernous room with her father and stepmother. They'd sat in the U-shaped grouping of couches in front of the fireplace and she'd showed them the ransom note, the dark hair in the baggie. Her father had seemed overjoyed at the prospect that Shane might still be alive.

But did he really feel that way? Or had it all been for show?

He was the one who'd suggested they involve Gage. She'd understood his desire to keep things quiet, to protect his legacy and to protect future leaders by not setting a dangerous precedent for making deals with criminals. But had he taken it a step further? Had he hired someone to eliminate her and Gage to ensure the ransom was never paid? So that nothing about the ransom ever made it into the media? Would he really trade his own daughter's life for his legacy?

Opulence surrounded her, enormous sums of money spent by a frugal man solely because appearances mattered. Appearances truly were everything to Earl Manning. And he, more than anyone, knew the public would look much more favorably on a grieving father than on a hypocritical former president who'd broken the rules and policies he'd touted his entire political career to ransom his grandson. Would he go so far as to hire someone for a bogus assassination attempt so he could later pin his daughter's death on similar zealots, out to hurt him by hurting his family?

She shivered and reflexively rubbed her arms.

"Harper?" Gage asked.

"Sorry. Did you say something?"

He smiled. "The past few weeks have to feel like the longest weeks of your life. You're exhausted, aren't you?"

Exhaustion didn't come close to covering how she felt. And she really didn't want to deal with her family once they got home. She was barely holding herself together right now.

"I guess I am. I could use a nap. So could you. At

least I got some sleep last night. You didn't. There are guest rooms in the back hallway beneath the stairs." She rolled her eyes at herself. "Why am I telling you? You know this house as well as I do."

"Thanks for worrying about me. I'll go to bed soon. But first, I'll escort you to your room."

"I grew up here. I think I can find it on my own."

His smile dimmed as he picked up her overnight bag, which he'd left in the foyer while he'd made sure there was no one waiting for them inside the house. "I'm sure you can. But with your sore ribs, I'd like to carry this up for you."

"Oh." Harper's face heated. "Sorry." What else could she say? Things were…awkward between them now. While he seemed to think he'd cleared the air, her heart had been shattered.

Gage followed her up the stairs, stopping at the open railing that ran about thirty feet across the gallery that looked down into the foyer. "You remember the plan I explained on the way here?"

"I remember. It's all set?"

"It is. I didn't want you to be surprised."

She headed down the hallway, stopping in front of the next-to-last door on the right.

Gage opened the door and set her bag just inside. "I hear cars outside. Your stepmom and siblings are probably here with the pizza they said they'd bring. I know it's closer to bedtime than dinner at this point. But you have to be hungry. I don't think you ate any-thing at the hospital today with everything going on."

"I really couldn't eat if I tried. Everything hinges on tomorrow, on the kidnapper making contact. And yet, nothing seems to have been resolved. What are we going to do when he sends the note with instructions for the exchange?"

"I think we're closer than you think to having the answers we need. Come morning, we'll have a plan in place."

"I hope you're right." She headed into the room and locked the door behind her.

BISHOP LISTENED TO the click of the lock then leaned against the wall outside Harper's door. Everything was set for tonight's plan. All the parts were in place. But he wished more than anything that he could undo so much of what had happened today.

He'd hurt her.

That was the last thing he'd ever wanted to do. Even when he'd thought she was the reason his career had imploded at the Secret Service, even with the resentments he'd carried for so long, he'd never wanted her hurt.

There was a time, when he was still assigned as the agent to protect her, that he'd considered quitting his job and exploring the attraction between them. His whole life he'd wanted to be a Secret Service agent. And yet the thought of a future without Harper in it had had him second-guessing whether his career mattered like it once had. But then things had gone horribly wrong and he'd turned bitter and resented her, blaming her for everything that had happened.

Yesterday, after seeing the picture of a little boy with a familiar birthmark, hope had flared inside him. A picture of a little family, the three of them, had taken root in his chest and expanded his heart. Everything he'd done since then had been with that picture in mind.

Then Mason's comment about him not being Shane's father had destroyed that dream. It had filled him with pain, and resentment that Harper had lied to him.

But she *hadn't* lied.

He didn't need a lab test to tell him the truth that he'd seen in her eyes when she'd told him about Shane. Even though he still couldn't remember that night in the pool house, he absolutely believed her about it. Because it was the missing piece of information he'd searched for all this time. It was the one fact that made what had happened all fit together. It explained how she could have been carrying his child even though he had no memory of sleeping with her. It also spoke to another question he'd never been able to answer—how she could have been seeing someone else without his knowledge as her protector.

Because of all the incidents back then where people had harassed her or threatened her over her father's political views, Bishop had stuck to her like glue. He knew who her friends were, who she'd associated with, and where she'd been at all times. He'd racked his brain over the years trying to think of who could have fathered her child and had come up empty. That was why he'd believed she'd lied about the pregnancy.

Now he knew differently.

He'd seen the pain in her eyes, heard the grief warring with hope in her voice as she'd pleaded with him to help her get her son back safely. Out of everything that had happened, that was the one constant, the one thing he knew to be true. She'd had a son. She'd named him Shane. And he was *their* son. His son. He never should have let the hurt and shock of Mason's announcement about the lab results sink in for even a moment. He never should have hesitated when Harper had asked him whether he believed her about the pool house. That one lapse had destroyed any hope left inside him that the picture of his future, a future with her, could be realized.

"Bishop? Harper? Are you up there? We've got the pizza." Julia's voice carried up the staircase from the foyer.

Bishop straightened away from the wall and headed for the stairs. He'd just reached them when Julia crested the top with her eleven-year-old son, Tyler, in tow. From the way he was yawning and rubbing his eyes, there was no question where they were going.

Bishop got down on one knee so he could look the little boy in the eye. "Hi, Tyler. My name is Bishop. I worked here a long time ago. You were only five. You might not remember."

Tyler stared at Bishop and cocked his head, as if studying him. "You took us to fly kites, me and Harper."

"Yes. Yes, I did. A few times." He smiled. "I'd forgotten about that. It's good to see you again."

Tyler let out a huge yawn.

Bishop laughed.

Julia tousled Tyler's hair and gave Bishop a wary look, no doubt remembering their unpleasant encounter in Harper's hospital room. "The nanny had already fed him but this little guy heard we were getting pizza and insisted that we stop and get him some chicken nuggets on the way. He's full, and sleepy, and about to pass out." She glanced down the hallway behind him. "Where's Harper?"

"Just as tired as your little guy there. She's not coming down for dinner." He stood, but kept his smile, not wanting his size to intimidate the dark-haired little boy who looked so much like his father. Tyler's wide-eyed stare seemed to indicate he wasn't sure about the big man standing in his house, even if he did remember flying kites with him.

Julia tugged on Tyler's hand. "Come on, kiddo. I'll see you downstairs, Bishop." She turned left and the two of them disappeared into one of the bedrooms that faced the backyard.

Bishop headed downstairs. He wasn't particularly hungry. But other than Dean, who'd claimed at the hospital that he needed to go back to the dorm for something, the rest of the people on Bishop's short list of suspects were all here. He might as well keep an eye on them to see if any of them slipped up and gave anything away.

When he entered the dining room, the sideboard had been set up with drinks, three different pizzas to choose from, and an array of real plates and silverware. The Mannings were probably the only people he knew who ate take-out pizza in a formal dining room on fancy china instead of on paper plates and with their hands.

Bishop kept silent for the most part as he ate a slice of pizza. He knew his earlier actions had everyone feeling unsure around him, not just Julia. But they seemed to gradually relax around him and the talk began to flow freely once Julia returned.

It was interesting to see the camaraderie between Faulk and the two women. Their relationships seemed far more casual than Bishop had allowed his to be with Harper when he was guarding her. In addition to trying to maintain his professionalism, he'd been struggling with his wild attraction to her. So he'd made a point of not joining her for meals very often in spite of her constant invitations. Most of the time he patrolled the property. And he'd slept in the pool house, relying on the security gate and alarms to alert him if anything happened at the main house.

Faulk seemed more like a friend than a bodyguard. And he'd chosen to stay in one of the guest rooms downstairs in the hallway beneath the stairs rather than the fully equipped pool house. That only made Bishop more suspicious of him. He could easily picture him and Julia, or maybe him and Cynthia, trying to make money off the ransom scheme, especially since Faulk and Harper didn't seem to share a close relationship.

Harper barely glanced at Faulk other than polite greetings whenever they saw each other. She'd been much warmer and more outgoing with Bishop than she ever was with Faulk.

When the leftover food was put away and the women headed up to their rooms, Faulk went outside to patrol the perimeter. Bishop headed into his guest room under the stairs. Much later, after Faulk had gone to his room and the house had settled down for the night, Bishop snuck out of his room and headed up the stairs.

A BARELY AUDIBLE click sounded from the direction of the bedroom door. Seconds later, a faint puff of air indicated the door had opened and then closed behind whoever had just snuck inside. It was too dark to see anything, but a whisper of fabric indicated the intruder was heading deeper into the room.

Heading toward Harper's bed.

Another second passed. Two. Three. The light flicked on overhead.

The man whirled toward the door then stopped and slowly raised his hands in the air.

Bishop stepped out of the open closet doorway, aiming his pistol at the man's chest. "The only reason I haven't shot you yet is because Harper isn't here."

Faulk's brows rose in surprise. He half turned to see the empty bed. "Where is she?"

"In a guest room, with a bodyguard. I took her usual bedroom to see if the person who was trying to kill her would take the bait. Looks like he did."

The blood rushed from his face, leaving him pale and gaunt-looking. "Kill her? I'm not trying to kill her. I swear it."

"Says the man who snuck into her room, in the dark, with a gun."

"The gun's in my holster. Part of my job, as you well know."

"Maybe I'll go ahead and shoot you anyway. Just be done with it."

"No, no, no." A bead of sweat popped out on Faulk's forehead and began to roll down the side of his face. "Let me explain."

"I'm waiting."

Faulk swallowed hard. "I needed to talk to Harper in private, away from her family. I wanted to warn her. And I couldn't do that in front of anyone else. I'd lose my job."

"Start making sense, fast. I'm losing patience. And this pistol's getting heavy."

"All right, all right. I was here a few months ago protecting the current president when he came for a visit. The whole family was here, all of the Mannings, including Harper. As you can imagine, there was a lot of security. Too many for all of us to be inside without being underfoot. So I went outside, patrolled the perimeter. On the way back, I heard a couple of people talking near the back kitchen doorway. I didn't want to intrude, so I ducked behind some shrubs to wait. I heard some things that…well, alarmed me. I mean, there wasn't a specific threat. Nothing I could really act on. But there was frustration, and anger."

"Directed at who?"

"Earl Manning."

"What's that got to do with Harper?"

"Everything. They were talking about using her to get back at him. But they went inside before saying anything else. I knew if I told Mr. Manning, he wouldn't take it seriously. He'd laugh it off. But the anger in their voices…" Faulk shook his head. "I felt it was a credible threat. But I had no proof. I didn't even know what they were planning, or when. So I did the only thing I could do. I asked for temporary reassignment to the Manning home so I could figure out what was going on."

"Thompson said you were reassigned because you screwed up."

"Yeah, well. That's Thompson for you. When has he ever not been a jerk? He's just ticked that I wouldn't tell him why I asked for the change in assignment. He's the last person I'd trust with my career."

"I'm with you on that. So why did you sneak in here tonight?"

"To tell Harper what little I know. I didn't tell her before because, quite honestly, I began to doubt myself. Nothing else had happened since then. But after hearing about those gunmen who went after you two, I'm convinced that I know who's behind it."

Bishop slowly lowered his gun. "Tell me exactly what you heard that night. And who you heard."

Twenty minutes later, Bishop carefully lowered himself into a wing chair in one of the guest rooms downstairs.

Across from him, sitting at the small desk by the window with his laptop open, Mason poured a glass of whiskey and offered it to him.

"No, thanks. I'm running on empty right now. It's going to be hard enough getting up in a few hours without alcohol in the mix."

"I should probably take the same advice, but I'm going to drink a glass anyway. Brielle's with Harper?"

"She is. Harper's not thrilled to have Brielle camped out on the floor by her bed while I took Harper's usual suite. But once she hears what happened, I have a feeling she'll be far more accepting of the inconvenience."

Mason took a sip from his whiskey and sat back. "So our would-be killer took the bait, only he wasn't our guy."

"I'm not marking Faulk off the short list just yet. But it seemed like he might be telling the truth."

"What about Thompson? He hasn't been sniffing around the Mannings since this started. But he was here a lot over the years for inspections and assessments while Faulk was assigned here. Could he be our guy?"

Bishop shook his head. "I wish I could say yes. Being arrested couldn't happen to a nicer person. But I called in some favors with some Secret Service agents

I still know. Thompson's schedule has taken him a lot
of places and his movements are pretty well accounted
for. I don't see him having the opportunity to set all
this up. Or, frankly, the motivation. His finances are
healthy. His investments are solid. He won't be hurting once he retires. I think we can safely cross him
off the list."

"That leaves us with the family."

Bishop sighed heavily. "Yes, it does. But even given
what Faulk said, we don't have anything to tie a bow
on this and offer it to Radley. He heard frustrations,
generalities. Nothing concrete. I think they were in the
early planning stages and hadn't really come up with
a strategy when Faulk overheard them." He checked
the time on the new phone he'd bought to replace the
one that had been destroyed in the creek. "It's really
late, or really early, depending on how you look at it.
I don't suppose the discarded soda cans we collected
at the hospital have already been tested? And that the
fancy lab you hired has results this fast?"

"For what I paid them, they should have had everyone on staff working all day and evening on our stuff.
If nothing else, I'd expect them to at least have blood
types by now, even if full-blown DNA takes several
more hours." He pulled out his cell phone and made
a call.

It took another hour to get preliminary results, with
final results promised by morning to be one-hundred-
percent conclusive. Still, the preliminary ones had a
high rate of confidence. When Mason clicked the
emailed report and displayed it on the screen, he and
Bishop both stared at it a long, solemn moment.

Mason finally shook his head in disgust. "You

were right to ask the Seekers to follow the family and get those discarded sodas for DNA testing. And I'm equally glad we got those additional blood tests." He shot Bishop a concerned glance. "You realize what this means?"

Bishop straightened away from the computer. "I do."

"I'm really sorry, Bishop."

He gave him a curt nod. "I hope Radley hasn't already gone to bed. If he has, he's about to be woken up."

Chapter Twenty-Two

Harper sat beside Brielle in front of the makeup mirror, but she couldn't seem to concentrate on whatever Brielle was saying. All she could seem to think about: this was the day the kidnapper was supposed to contact her. This was the day she was supposed to get Shane. She should have been home, *with Shane's father*, waiting for the mail. Instead, here she was at her father's home, feeling more alone and confused than ever, even though she was surrounded by other people. Everything was mixed up, and wrong, and—

"Earth to Harper. Are you even listening?"

Her gaze flashed to Brielle's in the mirror. "I'm so sorry. What?"

Brielle gave her a playful shove. "Girl, you missed my best analysis about the advantages of selecting just the right shade of blush. My talents are truly going to waste here."

She eyed her reflection in the mirror and shook her head. "Honestly, it doesn't matter how much makeup you goad me into putting on. I'm still going to be ridiculously pale."

"Yeah, well. Not everyone is blessed with my gorgeous brown skin." Brielle winked. "And I didn't goad you. I encouraged you. After all, if you want to catch a man like Bishop, you need the right kind of lure."

"I'm not trying to catch him."

Brielle grinned and gestured at Harper's face. "Now there's the right color of blush. Do that every time he smiles at you and you'll have him wrapped around your…well, whatever you want him wrapped around. Know what I mean?"

Her eyes widened in shock.

Brielle laughed. "Oh, come on. I've seen how you two look at each other when neither of you think the other's noticing. And I saw how dejected you were last night when you shut the bedroom door, with him on the wrong side of it. You're pining after him, whether you realize it or not. The heart wants what the heart wants."

Harper stood and washed her hands at the sink. "We're not having this conversation."

"Suit yourself. We can talk or not talk. Up to you. But breakfast is nonnegotiable. I'm starving. And until we catch the guy trying to hurt you, my existence in this guest room is our little secret. So I'm at your mercy. Go get me some food, Harper. Heavy on the carbs. The greasier, the better."

On impulse, Harper gave her a hug.

Brielle's eyes widened. "Not that I mind, but what was that for?"

"You're putting your life on the line for me. All of the Seekers are. 'Thank you' seems pretty lame. But I really do appreciate your help. Maybe I can sneak a cot in here tonight to make you more comfortable."

"It's all good, Harper. Thank me with breakfast. Don't dawdle." She winked as if to soften her words.

"I'll tell my stepmom I'm really tired and want to

bring my food back to my room and rest some more after I eat. Give me ten minutes. Tops."

"That's my girl. Extra bacon. I can smell that bit of heaven from here."

"You got it." Harper smoothed her hands down her navy blue slacks then headed to the door.

Suddenly Brielle was in front of her, blocking the way. "Hold it. Bishop just sent me a 9-1-1 text. Give me a second." Her fingers fairly flew across her phone as she exchanged messages with Gage. Finally, she shoved her phone in her jeans' pocket and checked the small pistol hidden in her other one.

"What's going on?" Harper asked.

"Unfortunately, it looks like breakfast is on hold. And me being here is no longer a secret. There's a meeting about to happen downstairs in your father's home office."

When Harper and Brielle began to descend the stairs, Gage was waiting at the bottom, watching them. Dressed in a fresh charcoal-gray suit, he was so handsome, her heart hurt to look at him. But as she drew closer, her steps slowed. He seemed so tired, his face drawn, his brow creased with worry as he watched her. She stopped two steps above him, clutching the railing as she met his eyes on even ground for a change.

"What is it? Did the kidnapper cancel the exchange?" She pressed her hand to her throat. "Shane. Is he okay? What's happened?"

Brielle stepped past her. "Is Mason in the office already?"

"He is. Just buy us a few minutes, all right?" He never took his gaze off Harper.

"Take as long as you need." Brielle hurried into the office and closed the double door behind her.

Harper twisted her hands together. "Mason's here? Why is your boss here, Gage?"

"Let's go into the family room. We need to talk privately before meeting with everyone else."

She glanced at the closed doors. "Everyone?"

"Your family, including your father. Dean, a few others."

"My father? He's here?"

"I contacted him late last night. He arrived a few minutes ago. Detective Radley's here, too. Don't be surprised if you see some uniformed officers through the windows. They're out front and a few out back. Along with some Secret Service agents, of course."

"Good grief. Why are all those people here? How are we supposed to make the exchange today and keep it quiet?"

"I'm about to lay everything out on the line, walk through what we've discovered. Get a few remaining answers I need to tie up the loose ends."

She tightened her hand on the railing. "You know who tried to kill us?"

He nodded.

"And…and Shane? What about him?"

He held out his hand. She grabbed it instinctively, her knees nearly giving out as he led her down the last two steps and into the family room on the opposite side of the foyer from the office.

As soon as he closed the door behind them, she turned to face him, her fingers splayed across his chest. The sight of unshed tears shining in his eyes as he looked down at her told her far more than any words ever could. But she still had to hear it out loud.

"Say it," she whispered, her voice tight and raspy.

"The plan to have me use your usual suite to draw out the killer worked, except it wasn't the killer who came into your room. It was Faulk."

"Faulk. But...if he's not the one who hired those gunmen, why would he sneak into my room?"

"He had suspicions and wanted to warn you. He witnessed things here last summer that had him worried, but with no provable facts. That's why he got reassigned. He asked to be reassigned, so he could find out what was going on."

"And you believe him?"

"The parts I could verify, yes. I was finally able to get someone to validate the facts about the reassignment. Everything else he said seems to fit with other things we've discovered. It paints a solid picture of what was happening. There are just a few questions remaining. This meeting brings everyone together so we can try to get those answers. But one thing is clear." He gently cupped her face in his hands. "I'm so sorry to have to say this, Harper. But the ransom demand was a hoax. There is no kidnapper."

She grabbed his wrists, holding on to him like a lifeline. "But... Shane. The ashes in the urn, they weren't real. Where—?"

"I don't know where he is, what Colette did with his remains. But there's no evidence that he's alive, that anyone has kept him all these years. We have to accept the facts. Our son died the same day that he was born. I wish with all my heart that I was wrong, that I could tell you he's alive. But I can't."

Harper squeezed her eyes shut. Her world tilted as he lifted her in his arms and carried her across the room. She buried her face against his chest and clasped her arms tightly around his neck as he held her, whispering sweet, reassuring words as he gently stroked her back. She wanted to cry, wanted to scream her grief and rage to the heavens. But the tears wouldn't come. Instead, a strange calmness settled over her. The grief was there, deep inside, battering at her wounded heart. But she realized she couldn't let it out, not yet. If she started crying, she might never stop.

She eased back in his arms to look at him. "I think that was my deepest fear this whole time, but I didn't want to admit it."

"That Shane was gone?"

She squeezed her eyes shut. "Yes. I wanted him back so desperately that I shied away from anything that didn't fit with making that happen."

Harper opened her eyes and stared up into his deep blue ones, looking at her with such concern. "I need to know everything you know. I need to know who did this, who hates me so much that they twisted the most precious thing I've ever had into a weapon to use against me." She pushed out of his arms and straightened. "Let's end this charade, right now. For Shane. For what could have been but never was. Let's do this for our son."

His Adam's apple bobbed in his throat as he searched her gaze. "Are you sure? I can take care of the meeting, and tell you everything later. You don't have to do this."

"I want to. Need to. Please."

He pressed a whisper-soft kiss against her forehead. "Then that's what we'll do."

WITH BRIELLE STANDING guard just inside the office doors to prevent anyone from leaving, Bishop stood shoulder to shoulder with Detective Radley and Mason, their backs to the fireplace. Facing them from the U-shaped collection of couches and love seats were Earl, Julia, Cynthia and Dean.

Bishop glanced at Harper. He was so proud of her for being so strong, but he wished she didn't have to be. She'd chosen to sit in a chair off to the side in spite of her father's and stepmother's attempts to get her to sit with them. She'd simply shaken her head, her back ramrod-straight as she'd kept her gaze focused on one person. Him, Bishop.

He gave her a nod of encouragement then addressed the others. "As you're all aware, the Justice Seekers, in conjunction with Detective Radley, have been working together to find out who hired the gunmen who went after Harper."

"And you," she said, her voice quiet. "They tried to kill you, too."

Cynthia piped up. "Why do you assume someone hired them? I thought they were some radical group out to hurt my father by hurting his family. The media said they were likely tied to the guy who tried to assassinate my dad."

Her father reached past Julia to pat Cynthia's hand. "Let Bishop explain why he brought us here for this meeting."

She huffed an impatient breath and crossed her arms. Beside her, Dean looked positively bored.

"That may well prove to be true," Bishop said. "The Secret Service is looking into that angle. The Seekers have been focusing more on the ransom demand."

Cynthia exchanged a confused look with Dean. "Uh, ransom? Hello? What are you talking about?"

"A couple of weeks ago, Harper received a letter, along with some hair samples, demanding ransom for her son, Shane."

At Cynthia's shocked look, he quickly summarized the events surrounding Shane's conception, the stint where Harper was in seclusion with the midwife, and the fact that Shane had died at birth. He pulled no punches, taking the blame for everything. And when Harper tried to interject a defense of him, he politely cut her off. No way would he let her blame herself for anything that had happened.

"Holy Hannah," Cynthia exclaimed. "So that's why you used to keep that urn everywhere you went. You told me it got dented and you got rid of it."

"I had to explain it being gone somehow. But when the ransom demand came, we needed to have the ashes examined."

Again, Bishop took over, bringing everyone up to date. "A lot of things have happened in the past few days to help us see a more clear picture of what's truly going on. That's why you're all here. Radley, Mason and I have a few more questions we need answered, and we're hoping you can help us." He motioned to Mason to take up the explanation.

"The first lab ran tests on the hair sample sent with the ransom note, as well as a hair sample that Harper gave the night she came here to tell her stepmother and father about the ransom demand. The lab concluded a mother-son relationship. They also tested the ashes in the urn and discovered they were likely fireplace ash, not cremation ashes. Based on that, it was reasonable to believe the ransom demand was legitimate. Former president Manning has been working since that time to liquidate assets to be able to pay the ransom on the designated date."

Julia smiled at her husband and rested her head on his shoulder. He took her hand in his and held it between them.

Cynthia looked at Harper. "Okay. So, apparently, I have a nephew I never knew about. And what? You guys are the ones in charge of paying the kidnapper?"

"That was the original intention," Bishop confirmed. "Things changed once the gunmen entered the picture. There was no way to keep this off either law enforcement's or the public's radar. But we've been trying to keep it out of the media as much as possible to give us the best chance at not spooking the kidnapper."

"You're still going to pay the ransom and get Shane?" Cynthia asked.

"No."

She exchanged a startled look with Dean.

Mason glanced at Harper and then explained. "I paid a private lab to conduct several tests on Harper's behalf. We provided a DNA sample from Harper and Bishop, as well as the hair sample allegedly from Shane that wasn't consumed in the first lab's tests. And since we had a short list of those who might possibly have found out about the pregnancy, about Shane, I had several of my Justice Seekers follow the three of you around yesterday to collect drink containers you discarded." He looked at each of them before continuing.

"The only person whose DNA we didn't collect was former president Manning's. But it turns out, we didn't need it. The lab's tests were rushed last night to provide preliminary results. We also had another lab analyzing the ransom note for DNA. Unfortunately, there wasn't any in a detectible amount. The person who sealed the envelope and put the stamp on it used a wet paper towel or something like that rather than saliva. But we did retrieve metadata from the ransom note."

Dean straightened in his chair. "What are you talking about? Metadata? In your earlier summary, you said it was printed, not emailed."

Bishop's jaw tightened. "Yes. It was. And the printer embedded data onto the page, providing the serial number and model number. We were able to trace the ransom note to the exact printer used to produce it. A printer in the library at Vanderbilt University."

Cynthia stared at him in surprise.

Dean swore and crossed his arms. "You're accusing me or Cynthia of printing it because we go to school there. You might as well accuse Mrs. Manning, too. She volunteers in the library." He gave Bishop a smug look.

"Well I sure didn't create a ransom note." Cynthia slowly turned her head to look at her mother. "Mom?"

Julia's eyes widened. "I had nothing to do with any ransom note."

Harper was watching her family, her face now pale, a haunted look in her eyes. But still she said nothing.

Earl's face was red but it wasn't clear whether he was angry or upset on Harper's behalf. "Mr. Ford, Bishop, Detective Radley, I hope you have something more than a piece of paper that supposedly came from a printer used by the community, not just students at the university, before accusing any of my family of being involved in this heinous crime against my daughter."

"Yes, sir," Bishop said. "We do. Quite a bit more, actually. But first, I need to ask Harper some questions. Harper, the night you came here with the ransom note and hair sample, can you walk me through the timeline? And who was with you, up until your hair sample and Shane's were given to the courier to take to the lab?"

She shifted in her chair and clasped her hands tightly together, looking at the floor as she spoke. "I called Daddy as soon as I got the note. He was here to visit Cynthia because it was her first weekend home. She'd moved out of the dorm for the summer semester. I drove straight here—I think it was about five. I know it was before dinner, because we ate together later and Julia always serves dinner at six."

Earl patted Julia's hand. "Yes, she does. Shortly after five sounds right. We went into my office to look at the note together."

Detective Radley pulled out his pocket notebook and pen. "Who is *we*?"

Earl's brows raised. "The three of us—Harper, Julia, me."

"Where was Cynthia? And Dean?"

Cynthia crossed her arms. "That's right. Try to blame whatever's going on, on the least favorite daughter and her boyfriend. Here we go."

Her father gave her a warning look. "I love all my children equally."

Cynthia rolled her eyes.

"Where were Cynthia and Dean?" Radley asked again.

Dean held his hands up as if in defense. "Don't look at me. I wasn't here. I still had a paper to finish that weekend. I was at my dorm."

Cynthia frowned at him. "Nice."

"What?" He blinked.

She shook her head. "I was upstairs, unpacking. I never heard anything about all this until today. I wasn't with them in the office when Harper came over. I only saw her once we went to dinner."

"That's true," her father said. "It was just the three of us in here, with the door closed. Julia got a plastic baggie from the kitchen and then used a pair of tweezers to pull out some of Harper's hair to make sure the root tags came with it. I'd called a lab I've used before and they said for a DNA test using hair we needed roots."

Radley jotted some notes. "And that same lab sent a courier to collect the samples?"

"Yes. He arrived about halfway through dinner. I'd put the samples in my desk drawer and came and got them, then gave them to the courier. That's it. Why does any of this matter?"

"Was your office door locked?"

"Of course not. I never lock it. There's no need. Again, why all these questions? What's it matter?"

"When Cynthia came down for dinner, where were the three of you?" Radley asked.

Harper stared at Radley then slowly looked at her sister. "The three of us were together in the office, then went to the family room. From there we helped each other serve dinner in the dining room. That's where we were when the courier came. We were together, the whole time."

Cynthia glanced back and forth from Harper to the detective. "Why does that matter?"

"It matters," Bishop said, "Because of all the DNA testing I mentioned earlier. Yes, the samples sent to your father's lab had a mother-son relationship. But the mother in question is your mother, Julia. And the son…is Tyler."

She blinked. "What? I don't understand. What are you saying?"

Her father's face had gone pale. He stared at Cynthia in horror. "I saw Julia take Harper's hair samples. For the lab to say the hair wasn't Harper's can only mean one thing—someone switched the samples."

"How could you do this to us, Cynthia?" Harper whispered brokenly. "You knew I would come to Daddy when I got the note. And you made sure you were here. You must have been watching from the gallery when we went into the study. When you saw Julia get the baggie and tweezers, you realized what she was doing. Or you listened outside the doors and heard us talk about it. You knew if they tested my hair against…" She briefly closed her eyes. "They would know it was a hoax if they tested my DNA and found no mother-son relationship. You did the only thing you could to salvage your plan. You got samples of Tyler's and your mom's hair from their hairbrushes and switched them."

Cynthia frantically shook her head. "No way you tested Tyler's DNA. I don't believe you."

"We didn't have to," Bishop said. "When the lab retested Shane's hair sample and Harper's blood, they confirmed a relationship. A *sibling* relationship. We knew that Shane's hair was really from her brother—which means it wasn't Shane's. It was Tyler's.

"There's no way anyone else could have switched the samples for the first lab. It was you, Cynthia," he charged. "By your own admission, by everyone's admission, the only people in the house that night were you, your father, your mother and Harper. Even Tyler was out. We verified that with the nanny this morning over the phone. Julia took him there so he wouldn't be here for the meeting with Harper. It's you, Cynthia. You're the one who set up the ransom hoax. And we believe Dean helped you."

"Me?" Dean squeaked. "You're crazy. It's all her. I'm not involved in this."

"You liar!" Cynthia yelled at him. "You're the graphics major. I'm not the one who Photoshopped that birthmark onto a picture. It was your idea! You talked me into it." She punched his shoulder.

"Why?" Harper's grief-stricken voice cut through the noise. The room fell silent and everyone looked at her. "Why would you give me false hope that my son was alive? How could you be so cruel?"

Cynthia's face turned red. "I wasn't trying to be cruel, Harper. I love you. I would never hurt you—"

"Stop lying. Just answer my question. Why?"

Cynthia stiffened. "You don't know what it's like being the stepdaughter, the only child in the family not related to the great 'President Earl Manning.' His blood is in your veins, in Tyler's, but not mine." She pounded her chest in emphasis. "Nothing I do is ever good enough for him. And while he spends thousands of dollars buying rare books to sit on the stupid shelves in this office to impress total strangers, and donates hundreds of thousands of dollars to charities, he leaves the rest of us to scrap for every penny we have. Do you know how embarrassing it is to have to turn down your friends to go to the movies or a concert because you don't have enough money to buy a stupid ticket? When your father is the former freaking president? Correction. Stepfather. No relation. And certainly never wanted."

She glared at Earl, who'd gone white as a sheet.

"I didn't want to hurt Harper," she continued. "God knows she's the only one around here who ever really cared about me."

"Cynthia!" her mother exclaimed.

"Oh stop it, Mom. All you care about is your stupid antiques and that ridiculous garden out back. How many freaking plants does one person need?"

Her mother blinked, her chin wobbling.

"Spare me the crocodile tears, Mom."

Cynthia turned back to face Harper, her own tears freely flowing now. "I'm not the stupid kid you thought I was when you told me that urn was a vase. I knew it was an urn. But I never understood why you hauled that thing around with you until I snooped in your room one day and found that baby book you keep."

Harper sucked in a breath.

"I'm sorry, Harper. I truly am. But, I mean, Shane died the day he was born. It's not like you had him for years and then he died. I didn't think it would hurt you that much by pretending he was alive. All I wanted was to make Daddy suffer. And get enough money that I could disappear, have a fresh start, and never have to see the disappointment in your father's eyes again whenever he looked at me."

"I loved Shane," Harper said. "I carried him for nine months, talking to him, singing to him, planning our future together. He was all I had of the only man I've ever loved. And it destroyed me when he died. How could you be so callous?"

Bishop stared at Harper, stunned. Her face had turned red and she refused to look at him, as if only just realizing what she'd admitted.

"What about the gunmen?" Radley asked. "Where do they fit in all this? Did you want to hurt your father by having his daughter murdered?"

"What? No. Of course not. We had nothing to do with that."

"I'm sure the search history on both your laptops will back that up."

"Whatever." She gave him a mutinous glare and looked away.

Radley shrugged. "The truth will come out soon enough. The hospital lab is running tests on the gunman who supposedly had a heart attack. And did I mention we're exhuming the midwife's body? Collette Proust? We're testing her to see if a poison could have caused her heart attack. My theory is that someone poisoned both of them to cause their heart attacks. We'll be able to prove who that person is once all the hypodermic needles from the medical waste container in the gunman's hospital room are tested and examined for any DNA."

Cynthia shook her head. "You're delusional. I was a teenager when Harper had Shane. I couldn't have killed some midwife woman. Why would I?"

"Teenagers kill all the time. It's a sad fact of our times."

She rolled her eyes.

"What about your boyfriend, Dean?" Radley asked, switching gears. "Is he the one who printed the ransom note?"

While Cynthia and Dean fell all over themselves to rat each other out, Bishop gave Mason a questioning glance.

Mason nodded, understanding what he was asking—whether Mason would work with Radley to try to get the details ironed out, and try to get a confession regarding the gunmen. Bishop had something far more important to take care of. Or someone. Harper.

He crossed to her chair and crouched until she looked at him. "Harper, there are a few more loose ends to take care of. Would you mind coming with me?"

She frowned, looking confused. But she nodded, let him take her hand and pull her to standing. They crossed to the door and Brielle silently opened it and then locked it behind them.

Chapter Twenty-Three

Of all the places that Gage could have taken Harper to tell her whatever last remaining devastating piece of information he thought she had to know, she felt this was probably the worst choice he could have made.

The pool house.

But as he shut the door behind them, cocooning them in together, an unexpected feeling of peace settled over her. The ups and downs, the fears, the horrific discoveries revealed in her father's study, all of it faded away.

Harper was transported back in time, almost six years, to this exact spot. This was where it had all begun. This was where she and Gage had created life. This was where Shane had been conceived. Her wonderful, precious little boy. And for some unknown, miraculous reason, she felt closer to her son at this very moment, in this place, than she had since the day he was born. It was as if he was here with them, trying to let her know that everything was going to be okay. That he was at peace. That he loved her.

"What other loose ends did you want to talk about?" she asked without turning around.

"Honestly? Nothing. I didn't want you to have to

witness what was happening next. You were upset enough already."

She twisted her hands together. "Thanks for that. What *is* happening next?"

"Radley's going to arrest your sister and her boyfriend. Mason's working with him to wrap up the details. Cynthia…she did searches on her computer about hiring a hitman. It appears that she and Dean were behind both the Gatlinburg assassination attempt, and hiring those men to attack you."

She let out a shuddering breath. "I can't…wow. I knew she had issues with my dad. But I never thought she'd take it this far. And I never… I thought we were okay. The age gap made it hard sometimes. And she always felt I got more attention. But we were…friends." She shook her head. "All this time she wanted me dead? It's hard to fathom."

He gently clasped her shoulders. "It appears your dad refused to pay her tuition for next term unless she got her GPA up. Her grades came in and…well, she was going to be on her own. She was furious and desperate for money. Killing him, then deflecting attention by making it appear someone was after the entire family, was her real plan. I don't know that she really wanted you killed. She might have hired them to make it look like they were trying to kill you but she was in over her head, hired the wrong kind of guys. It went too far."

"You really believe that? She didn't want me dead?"

"Honestly? I'm not sure. Just playing devil's advocate."

"To make me feel better?"

He slowly pulled her back against his chest, giving her plenty of opportunity to stop him. She didn't. He slid his arms around her waist and rested his cheek on the top of her head. "I'd take it all away if I could, to make you feel better."

She shuddered against him then put her arms on top of his. Closing her eyes, she tried to forget the bad and remember the good. In this place, with him here, holding her, she could almost picture the future she'd once hoped for. The three of them, a family.

"What are you thinking about?" His voice was hesitant, cautious.

"The day he was born. Our son."

"Tell me," he whispered.

She smiled. Remembering. "He had blond hair, a head full of hair."

"My hair was blond when I was born."

"Mine, too. I wonder if his would have turned dark like ours. I always assumed it would. That's why Tyler's dark hair in the baggie never phased me."

He kissed the top of her head. "Was he tiny? I always assumed he came early, because he was in distress when he was born."

She frowned and slowly turned around, tilting her head back to meet his gaze. "He never seemed like he was in distress to me. He seemed…perfect. He was full-term. A bit thin perhaps, but a healthy pink color. Long, lanky. He would have been tall. Like his father. Colette laid him on my belly while she cut the cord. He…he opened his eyes. And I swear he smiled at me, though anyone else would say I'm crazy to believe that."

Gage smiled, surprising her again with the unshed tears sparkling in his eyes. "I believe you. What color were his eyes?"

"Blue. Deep blue, like yours. I made him a baby blanket, with his initials embroidered on the corner. I tried to match the blanket to the color of your eyes. Silly, right?"

Ever so slowly, he threaded her hair back from her face, letting his hand linger against her neck when she didn't pull away. "That was sweet of you. If I had my preference, I would have wanted them to be a lighter blue, like his mother's eyes."

She smiled again, surprised that she could after everything that had happened. But the cruel, awful world beyond their door didn't matter at this very minute. All that mattered right now was him, her, and the little boy they'd created.

"Tell me more," he urged.

She reached up and lightly ran her finger over the small birthmark on his right cheek. "This. He had the same mark on his face, just a little higher than yours. I…made a sketch in the baby book." She swallowed. "My sister must have seen that and gotten the idea to Photoshop the picture."

He tilted her chin up. "Don't let her in. This is our memory, our moment with our son."

She stepped closer to him. He folded his arms around her, wrapping her in his embrace. It felt so natural, so…right, to be held like this. Because this was Gage. This was the gentle, kind, protective, wonderful man she'd fallen in love with years ago. The man she'd wanted for so long that she ached for him at night lying in her bed. A man who'd turned to her in his grief and let her soothe him, or so she'd thought at the time. She knew better now. But even though that memory, of them making love, was hers alone, she would always cherish it.

"How long did you get to hold him before Colette took him to the hospital?"

She tightened her arms around his waist. "Not long. Maybe ten minutes. He coughed, and started crying. Colette immediately grabbed him up and suctioned out his mouth. But he coughed again. I thought it was normal." She frowned. "I never realized he was in any kind of trouble. But she said he was having a hard time breathing, that she needed to get him to the hospital immediately. I kissed the top of his head. And then… he was gone. Just like that. She took him. And I never saw him again."

He rubbed a hand up and down her back in a soothing gesture. "I'm sorry, Harper. I didn't want to make you sad."

She shook her head. "It's okay. It was good to see him in my mind again, to share that with you."

He kissed the top of her head then pulled back. "Is it okay that I brought you out here? Everyone else should be gone by now. We can go back to the main house if you want while we wait for an update from Radley."

"It's okay. Honestly, I haven't been here since… since that night. I thought it would be a bad memory. Instead, it feels good to be here again. With you."

He looked around the large room that was part bedroom, part kitchen, part living room, just like it was all those years ago. "I don't understand why it's such a blank spot in my mind. I wish I could remember. I can promise you one thing, though. I'll never forget Shane, the memory you just gave me."

A single tear slid down her cheek. She wiped it away. "What happens now?"

"With your sister?"

"No. I don't want to talk about her. Not yet. I still love her, and I'll eventually forgive her, as crazy as that sounds. It will eat me alive if I can't figure out how to do that. But I'm not ready for that yet. I meant what happens now…in regard to Shane? I'm not naïve enough to think that he's alive. But why would Colette give me an urn full of fireplace ashes?"

"The Seekers are working on that. Tracing Colette's movements, interviewing anyone she may have interacted with back then, trying to figure that out. I promise I won't stop searching until I have all of the answers, until we can lay him to rest, together."

She tilted her head again. "I'm so sorry, Gage. About everything. I wish I could go back in time and—"

"Shh." He pressed a finger against her lips. "Don't agonize over what might have been, what could have been. It will make you a bitter person, and give you nothing but regrets. Believe me. I'm the champion at that."

She blinked. "You? What regrets do you have?"

He framed her face with his hands. "Don't you know, Harper? Haven't you figured it all out? I'm in love with you, have been probably since the day I was assigned to watch over you, when you were in college. It killed me that I couldn't act on that, ask you out, pursue you the way I wanted to. It's haunted me all these years that I didn't realize the truth, that you were far more important than a career.

"If I had realized that earlier, then maybe we'd have spent the past few years together, raising our son, instead of wasting all that time apart. I had myself convinced that you were the villain in my life, until I walked into that conference room in Gatlinburg. It took all of two seconds for me to realize I was still in love with you. But I was still holding on to my pride, my grievances. Well, I'm not going to do that anymore. I'm not going to waste another second." He lowered his mouth to hers in a whisper-soft caress, gently testing, tasting, teasing.

She'd wanted this, craved it, for so long. To have him here, telling her he loved her, wanting her as much as she wanted him. It was like a piece of a dream she'd barely glimpsed a very long time ago. But now the whole dream was within her reach. All she had to do was take it.

Harper slid her hands up his chest to the back of his neck and stood on her tiptoes, pressing her mouth to his. He groaned and suddenly she was in his arms, her legs wrapped around his waist. With one arm supporting her bottom, the other at her back, he turned, half stumbling as he carried her to the bed without breaking the kiss. His tongue tangled with hers, fanning the flames inside her.

This, this was what she remembered. This inferno of heat and passion that exploded between them the moment his lips met hers. She nearly wept from the beauty of it, the joy, the knowledge that her craving for him was about to be assuaged. Finally.

He sat on the edge of the bed, her body still wrapped around him as his hot mouth moved to her neck. He seemed to know exactly where to touch, where to press, where to taste. When his mouth moved to a sensitive spot just below her ear, she shivered. He kissed her hypersensitive skin then sucked. She almost fell out of his arms then and there.

Laughing, he stood, turned with her in his arms and then slowly lowered her to the bed. His blue eyes had darkened to the color of midnight. And all signs of amusement fled as he slowly covered her with his body, propping himself on his elbows to keep from crushing her. The feel of him, there, pressing her down, even with their clothes on, was almost more than she could bear. It was exquisite, magical, perfect.

He feathered his fingers through her hair, sweeping it back from her face, his gaze never leaving hers. "I've wanted this forever, wanted you, in my arms."

"That makes two of us," she said. "Don't stop now."

He grinned. "I have no intention of—" His phone buzzed in his pocket, startling both of them. His smile faded. "Don't go anywhere."

"You, either."

He pulled out his phone. But when he saw the screen, he bit off a curse. "Perfect timing."

"Ignore it, whoever it is."

He gave her a look of regret. "I'm sorry, Harper. It's Mason. He's says it's urgent. I can't ignore this."

She sighed as he rolled off her and stood. "I know, I know. It's just…like you said. Really bad timing."

He glanced up from the screen where he was typing a text, and winked.

Her stomach did a delighted little flip.

He shoved the phone back in his pocket then leaned down and pressed a quick kiss against her lips. "He's at the police station and needs me to look at some file on his laptop in the guest room, then call him. Hopefully, this will be quick. Wait for me?"

"I've waited for you all my life. A few more minutes won't kill me."

His hands shook as he cupped her face. "I think I've waited for you my whole life, too. I was just too stupid to realize it before." He gently stroked her cheeks and stared down into her eyes. "You are so beautiful." He gave her another kiss that ended far too quickly. Then he was gone.

Harper fisted her hands against the mattress in frustration, but she couldn't quit smiling. Things hadn't gone the way she'd expected, not at all. And there were going to be some really rough times ahead with her family. But she knew she wouldn't have to face it alone. Gage would be with her. Settling more comfortably against the pillows, she closed her eyes and waited for his return.

Thump. Thump. Thump.

Her eyes flew open and she sat up. What was that noise? She heard it again, a rhythmic sound, coming from outside. Crossing to the bank of windows that looked across the pool to the back of the house, she didn't see anything to explain the noise. The thumping sounded again, and she realized it was coming from the side of the pool house. She headed past the living room area to the windows there, looking out over the maze of oleanders her stepmother had planted over the years. It was a sea of green with white and pink blooms that had Julia blushing with pride every summer.

It took a moment for Harper's eyes to adjust to the bright sunlight, and then she saw her. Julia. Sitting in the dirt about twenty feet from the house, wearing the same dress slacks and blouse she'd had on earlier. She was digging around the base of one of her precious plants with a foot-long hand shovel. Weeding, or maybe thinning out overgrowth. Harper had never been much of a plant person, so she wasn't sure.

Puzzled that her stepmother wasn't at the police station with her daughter, it dawned on her that Julia was crying. Tears tracked down her cheeks, glinting in the sun. She wiped at her streaming eyes after every two or three stabs of the shovel in the dirt. Apparently, she was doing what she always did when the stress of the world was more than she could bear. She turned to her gardening.

With a heavy heart, and more than a little guilt, Harper moved to the side door and stepped onto the concrete path that circled the pool house. Not wanting to startle her stepmother, she quietly made her way between the rows of six-foot-tall plants, stopping several yards away. But her intended greeting went unsaid when Julia had a sneezing fit then cursed her allergies and wiped at her eyes again. She wasn't crying. And she wasn't weeding or thinning out the plants. She was digging something up.

A large metal box.

Where her movements had been methodical and measured before, now she was viciously stabbing at the dirt, hacking at the roots of her beloved oleanders, then frantically tugging at the box.

It jerked free, slamming against her face. She let out a small cry and fell back. The box fell to the ground.

Harper rushed forward. "Julia? Are you okay?"

Julia whirled around on her knees, her eyes wide with surprise. "Harper? What are you doing here?"

"I needed some time alone before heading downtown to see Cynthia." She frowned. "You're bleeding.

Your cheek is…" She stared at the box. It had come open and a delicate blue blanket spilled from the corner, satin initials embroidered on its edge: S.B.

Shane Bishop.

Harper's hand shook as she reached out and lightly traced her fingers across the monogram. "That's… that's the blanket I made for my son, for Gage's and my son. Colette wrapped it around him to take him to the hospital." Tears spilled down her cheeks as she stared at the blanket. Then she looked at the box again, horror making her shake as she mentally measured it.

Two feet long.

One foot wide.

One foot deep.

She started to reach for the box, but snatched back her hand. Her entire body was shaking. "My God. What have you done? Please tell me my son isn't in that box."

"I'm so sorry, Harper. It wasn't supposed to be like this."

A sob escaped Harper's clenched teeth. She dragged in several more agonizing breaths, desperately trying to make sense of what was happening. "What did you do, Julia? What in God's name did you do?"

"I'm sorry," Julia said again.

A tinny sound had Harper glancing up to see a metallic flash in the sunlight. She threw up her arms to try to block the blow from Julia's shovel. It slammed against her forearm, making her cry out and fall to the side. She desperately scrambled back. The next blow slammed against the side of her head. White-hot pain burst through her skull.

Everything went dark.

Chapter Twenty-Four

Bishop sat at the desk in the guest room, scrolling through the report while Mason and Radley spoke to him through the speaker on his phone.

"You're both right," Bishop said. "It's all too neat. Too perfect. Both computers with internet searches on hiring hitmen and assassins—and how to get away with it? I don't buy it.

"Cynthia's smart, always has been," he conceded. "The only reason she gets bad grades is that she's rebellious and doesn't want to do the work. And that boyfriend of hers is a computer graphics major. Why would they go to the trouble of printing the ransom note in the library so it didn't come back as having been printed on their own printers, then leave search histories in their computers that make it look like they're killers? If you ask me, someone else did those searches, hoping we'd find them. It's as if they knew what kind of evidence we'd need to tie everything up in a nice neat bow and handed it to us for an open-shut case."

"Agreed," Mason said. "That's why Radley and I are on our way back with some computer forensics guys and a warrant. We're going to look at any other computers in the house to see what else we can find. We think there's way more to this."

"I still think Cynthia's guilty," Radley said. "And her boyfriend. Of the ransom gimmick. But everything else? My gut tells me they've been set up to take the fall for the rest of it. The more I've seen them, talked to them, read reports from interviews with their friends and professors, they just don't seem organized enough or methodical enough to set up the assassination attempt or to hire those mercenaries."

Bishop sat back, steepling his fingers. "Cynthia was in high school when Shane died. I know Radley said teenagers kill—it's not unheard of. But I have a hard time picturing her doing it. I knew her back then. She was focused on weed and boys, period. Not to mention, there's just no motive."

"Someone else hired the assassin and the mercenaries," Mason said. "I think we agree on that."

"We do. The question is who, and why. Radley, have you gotten the results from the tests on the syringes from the hospital?"

"No, and it's not looking good. I don't think we can count on that to be our smoking gun."

"So all we really have at this point is a gut feeling, and a belief that a killer may have injected two people with something to cause a heart attack," Bishop said. "The labs haven't come back with any conclusions there, either?"

"In spite of our bluffing in the meeting at the Manning estate," Radley said, "that's not looking promising. Typical toxicology screens look for hundreds of drugs. Nothing popped up. I'm going to ask a professor at one of the local universities for suggestions of other things to look for, something that doesn't show up on normal tests unless you know to specifically test for it. We could very well be looking at real heart attacks. Seems oddly coincidental, but it happens."

Bishop had been staring out the window as he'd listened to them. The tall plants on the left side of the pool house seemed to go on forever. The same plants he'd seen at Harper's yard. He remembered her saying her stepmother had given them to her... Something was niggling at the back of his mind about those plants, something he'd seen on some forensics show on TV. He pulled the keyboard to him and typed a string into the search engine. "Hey, Radley. Can you tell me how Julia Manning's first husband died? I've got a hunch."

"I've probably got that right on my phone. I have a brief background on all our potential suspects. Hang on." A moment later he said, "Here it is. Well, what do you know. Heart attack. I think that coincidence theory is out the window at this point."

"I'm with you on that." Bishop pressed Enter and his screen filled with pictures of plants. He scrolled down to the bottom of the page. "Bingo! That's it. There's a plant that's highly poisonous and if ingested in large enough quantities can mimic the reaction of a drug that saves lives if someone has a heart attack. But if they don't have heart trouble, it will give them a heart attack."

"You're talking about digitalis?" Radley said.

"I am. Guess what plant mimics digitalis?"

"No clue."

"Oleander." His gaze shifted out the window. "And I'm looking at hundreds of them right now."

"Where?"

"The Manning's backyard. Julia Manning's garden is full of them."

"Great work, Bishop," Radley said. "If we can use Mason's lab for quick results, maybe they can look specifically for oleander poisoning with the gunman?"

"Of course," Mason said. "I can get Bryson to call his Paris contacts, too, and make sure they also test Colette's remains for oleander."

"If those both come back positive," Radley chimed in, "I'll see about exhuming Julia Manning's first husband. What about motive? Juries always need a motive and I'm stumped on this one."

"I'm blank on that one, as well," Bishop said. "But if she killed her first husband, what's to stop her from killing the second one? Maybe she got tired of him, who knows? But with Earl being so high-profile, and having a physical every year by the same doctor who gives the sitting president his physicals, I imagine she didn't think she could get rid of him by faking a heart attack."

"Divorce by assassin," Mason said. "And make it look like the whole family was at risk by having them go after Harper, too? To draw attention away from Mrs. Manning?"

Bishop unclenched his hands. "It's a theory. And it makes sense she'd go after her stepdaughter instead of her biological children. If you lay it all out, think it through, it's a macabre kind of logic. Cynthia creates the ransom hoax to get money. Julia decides that's the perfect diversion to allow her to get rid of Earl and frame her daughter."

"If that's the case, what about Shane? And Colette Proust?" Radley asked.

"The one thing that Harper and everyone else drove into us this whole time is how important the Manning reputation is to Earl," Bishop said. "When Shane was born, he was still in the White House, seeking a second term. What if Julia's the one who safeguarded his reputation? In her own sick way, maybe she thought if she eliminated Shane, and the midwife, then there was no chance of the truth ever getting out and potentially harming her husband's career. To a sane, normal person, it makes zero sense. But if she's a sociopath, with no conscience, who'd already killed at least once—"

"Her first husband," Radley said.

"Exactly. Killing again after that was considered a reasonable way to take care of a problem—in her mind. Killing an innocent baby, and the midwife, no big deal for her. It was a means to an end. Later, when she grew tired of Earl, killing him would be quick and easy and she'd still get his millions. Except that because of who he was, there'd be investigations. Cynthia's scheme gave her the perfect opportunity."

Mason swore. "And framing her own daughter didn't bother her at all. She truly is a nut job."

"If our theory is true," Bishop added. "It's still just that, a theory. We need proof, preferably before Cynthia is railroaded for murder."

"I'll get the lab on this right away," Mason told them. "Exhuming the first husband is the key. And I'll text Eli and Caleb to go to the hospital to hang in the hallway outside Mrs. Manning's room. The Secret Service agent assigned to watch over her is there to protect her, not to keep her from escaping."

"The hospital? I thought she was at the police station."

Radley answered. "She was so distraught on the

way to the station that Secret Service took her to the hospital. She's been sedated."

Bishop straightened in his chair. "Who's the agent guarding her?"

"I think it's Faulk," Radley said. "Why?"

Bishop shoved back from his desk and hurried through the main house. "If we assume that Julia injected the gunman at the hospital to make sure he wouldn't tell anyone that she'd hired him, how would she have known he was there so she could bring the poison with her? I didn't mention the gunman when I called the Mannings."

"Maybe she's crazy enough to carry the poison with her all the time," Radley said. "Or, what are you thinking? Someone else poisoned him?"

"No. I think someone else called her and told her about the gunman so she could mix up a batch of poison and bring it with her. He was sick that first day in the ER. She probably poisoned him the very first time she came to the hospital to visit Harper…

"For her to have come that first day, with the poison, she had to have been given advance notice that the gunman was there. She has to be working with someone else. I'm betting it's the same person who's been with her since he requested reassignment. He sounded believable about overhearing Cynthia and Dean talking about wanting to hurt Earl in some way, because he really did hear that conversation. But he used that information to try to frame Cynthia for murder, not the ransom route they eventually chose."

"You're talking about Faulk."

"Yes. I think he's in this just as deep as Julia. Mason, did you text Eli and Caleb already?" He yanked open one of the French doors off the back and jogged past the pool, heading to the pool house.

"I did. The hospital's not too far from the station. They were— Wait, Eli's texting me back now. Hang on."

Bishop shoved the door open and ran inside the pool house. The big bed to the left of the door was empty. So was the couch, and the kitchenette. He hurried to the bathroom. The door was standing wide open. "She's not here."

"Who?"

"Harper. She was supposed to be in the pool house." He ran to the front windows and looked out. Then he ran to the side windows.

"Bishop, Eli said they called the hospital. Faulk and Mrs. Manning never arrived."

"Why wasn't I told?" Radley swore. "I'll get my team looking for her right now. I'll get a BOLO out on her car. She didn't go back home?"

"That's what I'm worried about," Bishop said. "If she did, I didn't hear or see her." He spotted some broken plants in the otherwise pristine garden. He yanked open the door and ran outside.

"Bishop?" Mason asked. "What's going on?"

"I'm trying to find Harper. Mason—"

"We're almost there. I'll get the Seekers out there. I just texted Eli and Caleb. They're turning around now and heading your way."

Gage stopped in the middle of a row of oleanders, the blood draining from his face, leaving him cold as he looked at the ground that had been destroyed.

His hand shook as he spoke into the phone. "Radley, get your cops out here. Get the Secret Service. Get *everyone*."

"What's wrong?" Radley asked. "What have you found?"

"In the garden, beside the pool house. Evidence of a struggle. Broken plants. Footprints. I think they're Harper's. And someone else's. They're small. Probably Julia's." His heart seemed to squeeze in his chest. "There's blood. A lot of blood."

"Hold on," Radley said. "We're just down the street now. I can see the house."

"Harper. I can't…she can't—"

"Don't lose hope, Bishop," Mason said, his voice tight.

Bishop bent, studying the dirt. "There's a blood trail. It's faint. A few drops here and there. And, thank God, two sets of footprints. I think Harper's still alive." He hurried along the row of plants. Good grief, did this garden never end? He stopped every few yards, searching until he found another drop.

Finally, he reached the end of the row. The drops were long with a slight tail, indicating the direction the person was heading as the blood dripped from them. He continued off to the right, deeper into the estate, toward a stand of trees about thirty yards away.

"What's going on, Bishop? Sit rep!" Mason demanded.

Gage jogged to the trees then slowed to check the ground again to make sure he was going in the right direction.

"Bishop?"

"Give me a second." He turned in a slow circle, widening his search radius. Then he spotted it. Another drop, with an elongated tail, proving he was headed the same way as the injured person, presumably Harper.

"They haven't left the estate. Mason, the trail leads deeper into the property, toward the woods on the south side of the property." He shaded his eyes, scanning the trees and bushes a hundred yards away. Two figures moved in the shade, the one in front slightly hunched over, holding some kind of box in her hands. *Harper*. Behind her, Julia shoved her forward. The two of them disappeared into the woods.

Bishop took off running.

Chapter Twenty-Five

Harper shook her head, desperately trying to clear her vision. Her ears were ringing from the blow with the shovel. She'd thrown up twice already and was having an awful time just trying to keep from falling over.

Julia nudged her from behind, pushing her deeper into the woods. Harper stumbled, catching herself against a tree with one hand while keeping the precious box clutched against her chest with the other.

"I'm sorry, Harper," Julia said. "I shouldn't have hit you so hard. I never meant for you to suffer." She reached for her arm, but Harper jerked away.

"You never meant for me to suffer? You *murdered my son.*"

Julia dropped her hand, but kept the lethal shovel in the other hand at the ready. "You didn't give me a choice."

Harper stared at her incredulously. "What are you talking about?"

"The pregnancy. Your father's reelection was coming up and he was slipping in the polls. His entire platform relied on a show of strength and integrity. One little mistake could have cost him everything.

"I couldn't risk anyone finding out about you having

a child out of wedlock. So I bribed Colette to give me the baby as soon as it was born. I told her I would give him to a family in a private adoption. But of course I couldn't risk that, either. Someone was bound to figure it out eventually, especially with that birthmark on his face, like his father's."

She gave Harper a plaintive look, as if expecting sympathy. "He didn't suffer. I held my hand over his nose and mouth. It was over in just a few minutes. But Colette grew a conscience. She didn't trust me and demanded to see the baby. I had no choice. I went to her apartment right before she left for the airport, and made up a story about the baby being with a nanny. We talked over tea and I spiked hers with stewed oleander leaves. She agreed to be quiet if I sent her baby pictures soon. As far as I know, no one in Paris ever suspected anything when she died. It was a perfect plan."

Harper stared at her in horror. "Would you listen to yourself? You murdered my child. Then you murdered Colette. And you justify it because of a political campaign?" She pressed a hand to her throat. "Did my... did my father know about this?"

"What? Earl? Of course not. He's weak, always has been. He never would have gotten reelected if it wasn't for me." She prodded Harper with the shovel. "Hurry up. Head that way."

Harper wove her way between the trees, grateful they were close together so she could brace herself against them to keep from falling. She glanced over her shoulder. "Was the ransom your idea?"

Julia snorted. "That stupid plan? Of course not. My idiot daughter and her equally stupid boyfriend thought that one up all by themselves. I realized what was going on, of course, since I knew there was no child to ransom. I figured I'd take it as an opportunity.

"Earl's been talking to a divorce lawyer and doesn't think I know about it. I knew this day would come, so I've been stashing money away. A *lot* of money. But if I could have him killed, and you, too, I could blame it all on Cynthia when her ridiculous ransom plan fell through. I'd have gotten everything. But you ruined it by bringing your ex-lover into the picture. You and your father would both be dead by now if it wasn't for his interference. Now I have to go with plan B."

A familiar thumping noise sounded up ahead. Harper stumbled to a halt when she saw someone with a much larger shovel than Julia's, digging a hole in the ground.

He turned around, his eyes widening in shock when he saw her. "Harper?"

"Faulk. I should have known you were helping Julia. You've been her constant shadow for months."

He climbed out of the hole and tossed two large plastic bags onto the ground. Neat stacks of bills filled each one. Harper's fuzzy vision was useless for figuring out the denominations. But even if they were only twenties, or fifties, it was an enormous amount of money in those bags. Probably hundreds of thousands of dollars.

"It always comes down to money, doesn't it?" she accused. "My family trusted you. How could you help my stepmother kill my baby? Then hire those thugs to kill my father and me?"

"What? No, no, no. I didn't do any of that. I've been trying to talk her out of her crazy plans from day one."

Julia shoved her forward until she was just a few feet away from him.

"Day one?" Harper accused. "Was that before or after she murdered Shane?"

His face reddened. Then his gaze fell to the box in her hands and he wrinkled his nose. "Is that where you disappeared to, Julia? I told you to leave it. All we had to do was get our money and get out of Dodge."

"I was going to plant evidence in the box to make it look like Cynthia's the one who killed the kid."

"What good would that have done?"

"If she gets charged with our crimes—"

"Your crimes."

Julia narrowed her eyes at Faulk. "If she gets charged, I'm in the clear."

"Did you miss the part about them doing lab tests on the syringes from the hospital?"

She waved her hand in the air. "Anyone could have put a syringe in one of those medical waste things. Any lawyer could get that tossed out."

"If you're so sure you could beat this thing, why bring Harper here? Now you have a witness. There's no way out for either of us except to run at this point."

"Yeah, well. Like I said. I didn't expect her to catch me digging up the stupid box. I brought her with me to buy some time. We can keep her as a hostage."

He shook his head. "No way. She'll slow us down."

"Fine. What do you propose we do about her then?"

Faulk swore and drew his gun.

Harper gasped and stumbled back.

He gave her an apologetic look. "I'm sorry about this. I really am." He raised the pistol.

Bam! A gunshot echoed through the woods.

A red dot appeared on Faulk's forehead. His eyes

rolled up in his head and he slowly crumpled to the ground.

Julia shouted with rage and dove for the gun he'd dropped.

"Harper, move!"

Gage's voice galvanized her into action. She threw herself into the gaping hole that Faulk had dug and covered her head with the metal box.

Gunshots seemed to ring out all around her. Loud pings echoed in her ears. She squeezed her eyes shut, making herself as small as possible as she pulled her knees to her chest beneath Shane's box.

The deafening sounds suddenly stopped. An eerie silence fell over the glade.

A moment later, a puff of dirt rained down on her. She jerked back and opened her eyes.

Gage was beside her in the hole, his face pale. "My God. I thought you were…" He shook his head, gently tugged the box from her arms and set it aside.

"Is she okay?" Mason's face appeared above them, just past Gage's shoulder. Another familiar face joined his. Detective Radley.

"I think so." Gage ran his hands over her arms, along her torso, down her legs. They were shaking when he gently probed her scalp.

She winced and ducked away.

"Sorry, sweetheart. I'm going to get you out of here now, okay?" He scooped her into his arms and climbed out of the hole with Mason and Radley helping him up.

"Wait," she said, her voice groggy even to her own ears. It was so hard to stay awake. "The box. It's—"

"I know," he said, his voice hoarse. "Don't worry. Mason will get it for us. Won't you, Mason?"

"Of course." He hopped down into the hole. A moment later, he was back in front of them, his face pale. "I don't understand it. The bullets. There are holes all over the top. Nothing on the bottom."

"Shane protected me," Harper said, resting her head against Gage's chest. "He saved me. You both did. Father and son."

Gage exchanged a startled glance with his boss then turned and strode back toward the house.

Chapter Twenty-Six

Bishop helped Harper out of the wheelchair beside the last pew in the aisle. She wobbled and grabbed his arm to keep from falling.

He frowned as he steadied her. "You shouldn't have worn those dangerous high heels. Kick them off. The preacher isn't going to mind if you're barefoot. And if he does, who cares? There's no one else here to notice, and I'm fine with it."

She gave him a reproachful look and leaned past him to smile at the preacher waiting at the front of the little mountain church just a few miles from Bishop's home in Gatlinburg the two of them now shared. She looked up. "I care. I'm not going barefoot to my son's funeral."

"Our son."

She straightened his tie and smoothed his suit jacket. "Our son. Come on, Gage. Let's say our final good-byes to Shane."

He tucked her hand in the crook of his arm. "Are you sure you're ready for this? It's only been two weeks. A brain bleed is nothing to sneeze at."

"No. It's not. But you ordered everyone around at

the hospital like a general, so they took excellent care of me." She rolled her eyes. "I'm fine, *Bishop*."

"Are you always going to call me Bishop when you get aggravated with me?"

"Maybe."

"I prefer my fiancée to call me by my God-given first name."

To his horror, she blinked back threatening tears.

"Okay, okay," he said. "Call me whatever you like. I just want you to be happy."

"They're happy tears, future husband. But sad, too. I'm happy we're finally together, after all this time. And I'm happy to be able to put Shane to rest. But I'm sad, too. I wish my mom had lived long enough to know I had a son. And I wish my dad could have been here."

"We can postpone this if you want, wait until he's come to terms with everything that's happened and feels he can face the memorial service."

She shook her head. "No. He'll never feel right being here, not after what Julia did. He feels guilty that he didn't realize how unbalanced she was. Not to mention how much Cynthia was hurting, without him even realizing it. He's doing a lot of soul-searching right now, and he's focusing on helping Cynthia."

"That doesn't bother you?"

"Surprisingly, no. Not really. She's young, immature. She didn't realize how much she was hurting anyone with her scheme. I think it got away from her, became bigger than she expected. She admitted she never thought she'd really get the money. She was hurting, and wanted to hurt my father. At least she's finally getting what she really needed all along."

"What's that?"

"His attention. And love."

"You're an amazing woman, Harper Manning."

"No. I'm a blessed woman. I had a son I cherished. I spoke to him, sang to him, read to him, while I carried him for those nine months. And I got to look into his beautiful blue eyes and tell him I loved him when he was born." She reached up and cupped his face with her hand. "I'm also blessed to love one of the most decent, strong, smart, handsome, and honorable men I've ever known. I love you, Gage. With all my heart and soul."

He cleared his throat, twice, before trusting himself to speak. "I love you, Harper. More than you can possibly know. I thank God every single day that I got a second chance. And I plan on spending the rest of my life doing everything I can to make you happy."

She dabbed at her eyes then gasped in dismay at the makeup smeared on her fingertips.

He smiled and gently wiped the dark smudges from beneath her eyes. "Brielle wouldn't appreciate you messing up her hard work putting makeup on you this morning." He winked to let her know he was teasing. "You're beautiful, with or without makeup."

"Oh stop it. You're going to make me cry even worse."

He kissed her again, this time on the lips. "Come on. Let's head up the aisle before the preacher gets tired of waiting."

HARPER STOOD BENEATH the tent in the church grave-yard, her hand on top of the casket as she whispered her final goodbyes to Shane. Gage stood off to the side, thanking the preacher and the altar boys who'd served as pallbearers during the private ceremony.

Once the others left, he returned to her with the wheelchair. "Come on, sweetheart. This is the longest you've stood at any one time since you woke up in the ICU. You have to be exhausted."

She gave him a tentative smile and sent up a silent prayer that she'd made the right decision. He wheeled her around to face the parking lot and stopped. She didn't have to ask why. She knew why.

An older man with white hair and faded blue eyes stood about twenty feet away from them, leaning on a cane. He, too, was dressed in a suit, his tie slightly askew.

His mouth drooped slightly at one corner, as if he'd suffered from a stroke sometime in the past. But he stood straight and tall, a proud-looking man in spite of the anxious look on his face, the uncertainty in his gaze that was locked on his son like a laser.

As Gage's father limped forward, Harper turned in the chair. Gage's jaw was set, lines of tension crinkling around his eyes as he looked at her.

"Why?" His voice was a harsh whisper.

She winced then put her hand on top of his on the chair handle, relieved and hopeful when he didn't pull away from her touch.

"Because I've learned how precious and short life can be. I've also learned how special love is, and that it should be cherished, and nurtured, and never taken for granted. He loves you. And you love him. It's my fault what happened between you two. I don't know if this can be fixed. But I know I owe it to you to at least try."

BISHOP LOOKED DOWN at the woman who meant more to him than breathing. He ignored his father who'd stopped just a few feet away. His annoyance that Harper had contacted his father had evaporated the moment she'd looked up at him with those gorgeous light blue eyes of hers. She had a pure, true heart.

Even though he didn't want this, he knew she'd set up the meeting because she cared, because she loved him. And he didn't want her to ever feel guilt again about anything in his past. He squeezed her hand and tried to reassure her. "It's not your fault, Harper. It never was. It's his."

"Listen to what he has to say. That's all I ask."

"I already did. Years ago." He finally met his father's gaze. "He made his feelings perfectly clear. And he told me he never wanted to see me again."

His father's chin wobbled as he drew a bracing breath. "What I said that day was foolish and wrong. I've regretted it every day since. But by the time I got over my stupid pride and pushed past the grief that was still eating me alive, I couldn't find you. I tried. I went everywhere, called your phone. But your number was out of service. You were gone. Vanished."

Bishop frowned. "You went looking for me?"

"Two weeks after our fight. And for months after that. No one I talked to knew where you were."

He'd left Tennessee within days of the fight with his father. He'd sold his expensive smartphone, opting for a much cheaper one that wouldn't drain his savings while he tried to find a new way to make a living. If his father had tried to find him, unless he'd hired a private investigator, there really hadn't been any way to track him down.

"Fair enough," he grudgingly allowed. "But you being here now, as if you actually care, means nothing."

Harper gasped.

Bishop threaded his fingers through hers. More than anything, he didn't want to hurt her, or even to disappoint her. That was the only reason he hadn't walked away from his dad, that he was still standing there. He was doing this for her. But, as she'd said, he didn't know that this could be fixed.

"You're only here now," Bishop continued, being brutally honest, "because Harper told you the full story. She told you that I was drunk with grief over Shane the night we made love. That even to this day, I have no memory of the night we conceived our son, which is why I refused to stand up as his father when I learned she was pregnant. Not because I had no honor, as you accused me that day. I didn't have all the facts. And I was foolish enough not to trust her." He waved his hand dismissively. "Doesn't matter. Harper and I have made our peace. It's not for you to forgive or not to forgive."

His father's brow wrinkled in confusion. "Son, I'm not even sure what you're talking about. Harper didn't tell me about you being drunk, or anything else. She just told me about…about your child, my grandson, that he'd died at birth. And that you were holding a memorial service. I understood it was private, but I asked if I could be at the graveside afterward, to pay my respects—to him, and his parents."

It was Bishop's turn to be confused. "Then, you're not here to forgive me?"

The elder Bishop stepped forward and clasped his son on the shoulder. "It was never my place to forgive or not to forgive. My job, as your father, was to love you unconditionally. And I completely failed in my duty to you. I said some awful things that day. But I didn't mean any of it. I do love you, always have, no matter what.

"I'm here, as I said, to pay respects to my grandson. But I'm also here to beg *you* to forgive an old man who has nothing but regrets for what he did to you. I love you, son. What can I do to try to make it up to you?"

Bishop slowly shook his head in wonder. "Just love me, Pop. That's all I ever wanted." He stepped forward and clasped his father in a tight embrace.

Harper was crying like a watering hose when the two men finally stepped back.

Bishop grinned and motioned toward her. "Dad, meet my weeping soon-to-be bride, the love of my life, Harper Manning."

She gave Bishop a playful shove and wiped at her tears.

His father wiped at his own tears before offering a hand to Harper.

She motioned for him to come closer and she hugged him instead.

When his father stepped back, Bishop gave Harper a soft kiss on the lips and whispered in her ear. "Thank you for giving me back my family, for *being* my family. You're my everything."

She gave him a tremulous smile. "I love you, Gage Bishop."

"I *adore* you, Harper soon-to-be Bishop." He moved behind the chair and grabbed the handles. He smiled down at her as he spoke to his father. "Come on, Dad. You can ride with us to our home. We'll come back later for your car. We have a lot of catching up to do. To start, Harper and I will tell you all about your grandson. And how he saved his mother's life."

* * * * *

Look for the next book in award-winning author Lena Diaz's The Justice Seekers series when Deadly Double-Cross *goes on sale in June 2021.*

And don't miss the previous books in the series:

Cowboy Under Fire
Agent Under Siege

Available now wherever Harlequin Intrigue books are sold!

The narrow mountain road ended at the edge of a rock cliff. It wasn't as if Ford Cardwell had forgotten that. No, when he saw where he was, he knew it was why he'd taken this road and why he was going so fast as he approached the sheer vertical drop to the rocks far below. It would have been so easy to keep going, to put everything behind him, to no longer feel pain.

Pine trees blurred past as the pickup roared down the dirt road to the nothingness ahead. All he could see was sky and more mountains off in the distance. Welcome back to Montana. He'd thought coming home would help. He'd thought he could forget everything and go back to being the man he'd been.

His heart thundered as he saw the end of the road coming up quickly. Too quickly. It was now or never.

The words sounded in his ears, his own when he was young. He saw himself standing in the barn loft looking out at the long drop to the pile of hay below. Jump or not jump. It was now or never.

He was within yards of the cliff when his cell phone rang. He slammed on his brakes. An impulsive reaction to the ringing in his pocket? Or an instinctive desire to go on living?

The pickup slid to a dust-boiling stop, his front tires just inches from the end of the road. Heart in his throat, he looked out at the plunging drop in front of him.

His heart pounded harder. Just a few more moments—a few more inches—and he wouldn't have been able to stop in time.

His phone rang again. A sign? Or just a coincidence? He put the pickup in Reverse a little too hard and hit the gas pedal. The front tires were so close to the edge that for a moment he thought the tires wouldn't have purchase. Fishtailing backward, the truck spun away from the precipice.

Ford shifted into Park and, hands shaking, pulled out his still-ringing phone. As he did, he had a stray thought. How rare it used to be to get cell phone coverage here in the Gallatin Canyon of all places. Only a few years ago the call wouldn't have gone through.

Without checking to see who was calling, he answered it, his hand shaking as he did. He'd come so close to going over the cliff. Until the call had saved him.

"Hello?" He could hear noises in the background. *"Hello?"* He let out a bitter chuckle. A robocall had saved him at the last moment, he thought, chuckling to himself.

But his laughter died as he heard a bloodcurdling scream coming from his phone.

Don't miss
Trouble in Big Timber *by B.J. Daniels,*
available June 2021 wherever
Harlequin Intrigue books and ebooks are sold.

Harlequin.com

HIEXP0521